MW01147066

LACE AROUND THE MOON

The second Novella and Prequel to
The Berry-Picker House

Mary Pierre Quinn-Stanbro

NFB Publishing
Buffalo, NY

NFB
NFB Publishing/Amelia Press
119 Dorchester Road
Buffalo, New York 14213

For more information visit Nfbpublishing.com

TABLE OF CONTENTS

DEDICATION

This story is dedicated to Amelia (Molly) Yost, Raczka, Sniegowski, my great-grandmother and Eleanor Shear, my grandmother. It is to them I attribute my strength and determination. These two women are the strongest I have ever had the privilege of knowing and being loved by. What I have learned from them is that, "Strong women's voices are the ones that are actually heard."

Special thanks to:

Michael Marcklinger, Media Coordinator

Michael Nico Nostro, Graphic Designer

A portion of the proceeds from this book will go to:

Iron Island Museum, Buffalo, NY

Please Visit Lacearoundthemoon.com

REFLECTIONS

"Laissez les bons temps rouler!"

I remember how that was always my favorite saying. I could never seem to get it out of my mind but with all that had happened it didn't ring true with me at this point in my life. I was not in the mood for "letting the good times roll" as I didn't feel there were to be any more good times for me. I was heading back to New Orleans after Phillip's trial, death and burial. I needed to get back to my little cottage. It wasn't much, but it was mine and I needed to see my friends and feel the embrace of the Crescent City—my city—the city I had been gone from for far too long. While on the train, I reminisced about all that happened over the past four months and how I got to experience love and love lost. I realized that I truly did love Phillip Wilcox even with all his faults and I was so sad to think that the letter writing relationship we had cultivated and cherished over the past 17 years had come to its end. I was thinking about how just hours earlier I had been in the Berry-Picker House and had left my message on the wall. I was overcome with emotions and my tears flowed as I softly sang my song *Lace Around the Moon* very quietly to not disturb the other passengers on the train. I remembered exactly how the song became mine and what was all entwined in the words and meanings and what it meant to me—it was my life. I could also still smell the sweet, thick aroma of the grapes that I first experienced when I first went to be with Phillip during the harvesting season. I could taste them in my mind and the taste was bittersweet. I was resting my head on the glass pane window in the area where I was seated. I turned my face and saw my reflection. It was like I was looking into a mirror. I was actually startled. I saw how gaunt and drawn my face had become from the ordeal of the past four months. I needed to see a different person in this glass reflection and I realized I was the only one who could change that.

My mind continued to wander and my heart continued to crumble. It was so strange how it came to me. I asked myself the question—"Pierre, what would it take to make you happy?" I heard myself actually say out loud—"To be with my son." It was then that I decided that when I got back to New Orleans, I was going to find my son. The son that I had given up when I was 14. The circumstances of how he came to be my son no longer mattered to me. He was my son, of my loins and I felt the strangest sense of entitlement and fortitude. I was going to find him this time. I had tried years ago to find him, but when that did not happen, I lost hope and gave up. I had to do that to survive and just get by. Of course, my feelings of insecurities quickly followed my staunch determination to find him and dare hope for some type of relationship with him. But the words from my song rang true—"At times we went our separate ways, but that was just a passing phase." I knew that 40 some years was more than just a passing phase—but all things are relevant. To me the years didn't seem to matter anymore. I remembered many years ago when I asked God to send me someone to love and to love me and he sent me the man whom I thought was the love of my life. But now I started thinking that perhaps he was not God's answer to my prayers. It continued to become even clearer— the person I have been looking for most of my life was actually my son.

It was a very long journey home, but I was getting excited to touch my feet down on New Orleans soil. I had planned to get a ride back to my cottage by way of one of the men who would wait for people arriving at the terminal who may need a ride. I knew several of them and was so looking forward to getting my bags and going home. I knew the first thing I would do would be to pour a whiskey—neat, sit in my courtyard and look up to the moon and let my heart and soul heal over the many drinks

I planned on having. I didn't want to even contact any of my friends. I just wanted to be by myself.

Boy was I in for an unexpected homecoming. As the train slowly rolled up to my stop, I couldn't believe what I saw! There were many people there holding up paper signs that read, "Welcome home Pierre!" I was confused and didn't understand how all these people, most of whom I didn't recognize, could be there for me? I hesitated while stepping down the stairs with the assistance of the conductor. When my feet touched the ground, Irene and Dee were there with welcoming arms. I hugged them tightly and said, "I don't understand all of this?"

Irene said over the roar of the welcoming crowd, "While you were away, your song *Lace Around the Moon* has become a number one seller! Pierre, you are famous and all of these people are here to wish you the best and let you know we love you and appreciate your love of New Orleans. You are truly a New Orleans gem!"

How could this all be? For a brief moment I thought back to almost fifty some years ago when these two same women were waiting for my arrival after I had partook on a different train ride. The train ride that took my life in a different direction. How things have changed and how time has gone by.

After I got over my initial shock and thanked those who were there to greet me, I was approached by a young man. He came up to me and stuck out his hand for a hand-shake.

"Good evening Miss Pierre, my name is Gregory Baynes," he said. "I am a local reporter from the *New Orleans Observer* and I would be honored if you would consider letting me do an interview with you. I would like to do a story on your life, the success of your song *Lace Around The Moon* and about *The Berry-Picker Murder Trial*. It will be quite in-depth and it will run for a couple of consecutive weeks depending on how much you are willing to share with me."

I was dumbfounded and had to say that this was all too much for me right now. I needed to get back to my little home and unpack and get myself together.

"I understand," the reporter said. "Can I meet with you tomorrow?"

"I'll need a couple of days to get things squared away and to think about your offer," I said.

Baynes asked if he could come to my cottage in three days? "Yes," I replied. "I'm not committing to anything at this point, but you can come over and we can talk about your offer."

That night when I arrived home, I was amazed to see all types of notes and mail that had been slid under my door. There had to be 20 sheets of paper and just as many envelopes. I gathered them up and grabbed my bottle of whiskey from under the cupboard and headed out to my courtyard. I started to open the envelopes. There were bills in the pile and some congratulatory notes on the success of my song, but what was in one of the envelopes was something I had never even allowed myself to dream of. It was from an attorney's office representing the record company that I used many years ago when we recorded my song. It was a check for $5,000!

I was trembling thinking of how could this possibly be for me? In my confusion from seeing all the people at the train terminal when I arrived back in New Orleans and Mr. Baynes' proposal, I never let it sink in what Irene had said to me. I remember she said that my song *Lace Around the Moon* had become a number one best seller and she obviously was not joking. I had finally come into my own!

I thanked God out loud and said, "I'll be damned, I never thought this would happen for me. I really am now getting recognition for all my years of hard work and for the sacrifices I have made. Thank you for never giving up on me and for making this dream come true. But now dear Lord, there is one other request I must make: please help me to find my son."

I thought that now that I would have financial stability and even extra money, this could possibly happen. I decided I would go along with the reporter's offer. I would let him interview me as I saw that as my way of possibly reconnecting with my son. I was going to use the reporter for all I could get out of him.

For the next two days, I collected my thoughts and emotions and decided on some of the things I would share with Mr. Baynes. I was determined to be in control of this interview and was even finding myself a bit defensive about the entire ordeal. But I just kept on telling myself that this may be the only way I could find my boy and I knew then and there that I would do whatever it took to someday be looking up at the moon, holding my son's hand and singing the words to *Lace Around the Moon* to him. I was on a mission.

Mr. Baynes came over to my cottage as we had agreed upon. I asked him to sit down at my table. On the table were two glasses and a bottle of whiskey. I poured us each a glass and handed him one.

"Oh no thank you, I really shouldn't drink while I am working," he said.

"If you want to be working with me on this interview, we will drink so get used to it," I replied. "Besides Prohibition is over!"

We clinked glasses and I said, "To a working relationship that I hope will benefit both of us." He seemed so young and inexperienced, but I felt I had to give him a chance at this as I was banking on having a return on this investment. He asked what it was he was drinking? I told him it was whiskey neat—my drink of choice. At first, Mr. Baynes did not like the taste of the husky whiskey on his tongue, but as the glasses of the serum went down his throat over those initial four hours, he seemed to grow fonder of the drink. After we finished the bottle of whiskey that afternoon into the evening, Mr. Baynes said he had to be going. He was stumbling a bit, but I was proud of him for how well he could hold his liquor. From that moment on, I felt we could become friends down the line. I too was a bit drunk from the liquor, but it only helped to reinforce my mindset and provide clarity about my son—it didn't matter who the father of my son was—it was that he was of my flesh, of my blood and from my body. I had to find him and claim him as my own. For most of my life, I was looking for others to make me unfrozen. I now realized that I had to be the one to thaw myself out.

Mr. Baynes and I agreed to meet the next morning at 10 a.m. at Jackson Square. This was the place I felt most at home in New Orleans. It was the place where so many life altering experiences happened to me. I thought it would make the most sense to meet there as it was the place that seemed to calm and heal me. I arrived five minutes early and he was already sitting there with his briefcase, tablet and pencil. He didn't look at all hung over or under the weather. He asked me if I wanted to go over to the little café to the side of the Square for a coffee or tea. I told him I appreciated the offer, however, I really wanted to get started on the Interview. He said he understood and suggested the way to get things going would be for me to just think back to when I was a child. To think back to when I was very young and start my story there. I agreed that I liked that idea and the thing I liked even more was that he went into his briefcase and pulled out a paper bag and handed it to me. Inside was a bottle of whiskey and two small glass. As I said, I believed this was going to develop into a friendship. I sat on one side of a park bench and Mr. Baynes sat on the other. I closed my eyes and inhaled deeply and let out the air and hoped I would be able to get through this ordeal. I let my shoulders that were uptight and tense, drop. I went into a calm place in my mind and I was surprised how the words just started to flow...

CHRISTMAS DISHES

I truly loved my mother and I believed she truly loved me. While I was growing up, we did many things together such as baking and cooking. However, the thing we loved to do the most was sing. My mother's name was Amelia but everyone called her Meils for short. She could play the piano and although her voice was not as strong and beautiful as mine, she could sing with such sweetness in her voice. For the Christmas Holidays, we would always have friends and neighbors come to our beautiful home for wonderful brunches and dinners. Many people came for the food, but they also came for the entertainment of my mother playing the piano and her and I singing popular songs from the mid 1800's. I do remember how in anticipation of these holiday parties, my mother would take out her special dishes that she only used at Christmas. They had been passed down to her from her own mother. She would gently take them out of the boxes and have the servants wash and dry them all the while asking them to please be careful with them. She loved those dishes. We made a whole evening of singing and setting the table. That is one of my most cherished moments I still keep with me. I remember when I was 12, I wrote a poem for my mother about her precious dishes and gave it to her that year for Christmas. I asked her to please read it alone in private. She did and she came to my room and she was crying. She said it was the most beautiful gift she had ever been given because it came from me and from my heart. That year at our Christmas Dinner Party, she asked me to please recite it.

Christmas Dishes –

Another year around the holiday
  table,
she looks around and thanks God she
  is still able
to use her Christmas dishes for yet
  another season.
Perhaps at times it has been for selfish
  reasons.
To her they simply mean so much
and with her extra loving touch,
she softly lays them gently down,
longing to have family and friends all
  around.
With these Christmas dishes,

all she wishes
is for another year with them all.
Life hasn't been easy, but she still
        moves forward standing strong,
        standing tall.
With these Christmas dishes,
she also wishes for relief from her pain.
Since having lost loved ones, makes it
        hard for happiness to remain.
The love she has for her family and
        friends will be what keeps her
        going through the
        years, until the years end.
Sometimes there may be one less place
        to set,
but she tries to think of that without
        regret.
Knowing that the same plate may have
        been used by ones missing,
is her Christmas gift – thoughts of
        reminiscing.
The food is not all that matters,
but that they have chosen to gather.
The meal is what unifies,
but these Christmas dishes are the
        bond that ties.

With these Christmas dishes,
all she wishes
is for another year with them all.
Life hasn't been easy, but she still
moves forward standing strong, standing
tall.
With these Christmas dishes,
she also wishes for relief from her pain.
Since having lost loved ones, makes it
hard for happiness to remain.
The love she has for her family and
friends will be what keeps her
going through the
years, until the years end.
These dishes are a blessing that she
loves to share.
Using them is her way of showing that
she cares.
Thoughts of her children one day using
them lightens her soul,
So keeping them with family is her
main goal.
Even when they crack and they break,
and it makes her heart sad and ache,
to her they are still a treasure.
Their worth is not even possible to

> *measure.*
> *With these Christmas dishes,*
> *all she wishes is for another year with*
>   *them all.*
> *Life hasn't been easy, but she still*
>   *moves forward standing strong,*
>   *standing tall.*
> *With these Christmas dishes,*
> *she also wishes for relief from her pain.*
> *Since having lost loved ones, makes it*
>   *hard for happiness to remain.*
> *The love she has for her family and*
>   *friends will be what keeps her*
>   *going through the*
> *years, until the years end.*

All the people present told me how they loved the poem and thought that I should put it to music so that it could one day be a song. I didn't think of that possibility when I wrote the poem for my mother, but after hearing all of their positive feedback, I thought that maybe some-day when I was older I could perhaps do exactly that. I remember growing up in the Diamond Dust Plantation House. It was wonderful. I had the finest of clothes and toys. My stepfather was so good to me and that made my mother very happy. She thought it was so endearing of him to want to comb my hair every night before I went to bed and tell me little stories. He always wanted me around him at all of the social gatherings they had. He loved that I could sing and he paid for me to have voice lessons. He would always make a fuss about me when I would perform for all of his and my mother's friends and neighbors and at church. My life was like a dream.

Around the time I was twelve, people really started to listen to my singing and the applause and hand clapping they gave me after I performed was so wonderful and rewarding to me. I knew I had a gift from God and that I should do something with this gift. My life was perfect until I turned 13.

It was after that special Christmas with the special dishes and the special poem I wrote for my mother that things started to change. My mother came down with Consumption or Tuberculosis and things from that moment on were never the same for me. I lost my childhood innocence and was forced into womanhood far too soon.

BE-JEWLED

In my mind, I called my stepfather "D". That was the nickname I gave him because he was the devil. His actual name was Damas DuMonde. I called what he did to me "ravaging." It started when I was 13. I had developed early and had a voluptuous body for a 13-year-old. Each time I was ravaged by him, what I did to protect myself—protect my sanity that is—is I made up a movement that I called "frozen." What I would do was start at the top of my head with my open hand and move it over my face, down over my heart and down past my private parts and chant three times, "frozen, frozen, frozen." This is what would get me through all the hard times in my life. I froze myself. It was my "frozen ritual."

After each of these ravagings, he would give me a beautiful piece of jewelry. I didn't know if he did that out of guilt, or by him requesting that I wear the latest piece he gave me to our next social event that he was able to relive his thrill. My mother thought nothing of it or so I thought, as she always commented on how beautiful each piece was in her labored breath. I so hoped my mother didn't know what he was doing to me because the only thing harder to accept than the ravaging, would be that she did. I think "D" started ravaging me because he could no longer do that to my mother. He lost interest in sex with my mother as she was becoming more frail with each passing month from the T.B. Her sickness was draining her and taking away her very essence. Her eyes looked like sunken in oyster shells. They were gray and black and she looked so sad. Her once beautiful hair had lost its sheen and laid around her head like straw. The disease made it difficult, if not impossible, for her to do any daily tasks around the house and as time went by, she could no longer even bathe or dress herself. We had servants to tend to those matters but the servants did not provide "D" with the one thing he craved most—sex. I believe that in his twisted mind he thought that since my mother could not perform her wifely duties, that responsibility was passed down to me. He was a powerful man and had taken care of my mother and I since my birth father died several years earlier when I was just three. My father had worked for "D" as his Plantation Manager.

We lived in a cottage on the property and it was nicely furnished and clean. My mother saw to that. However, it did not have any of the opulence of the main Plantation's home. In the beginning, "D" was very good to my parents, especially my mother. But I heard stories as I was growing up that perhaps my father's accident on the horse may not have been an accident at all. People said that when "D" saw something he wanted—he took it. Rumors were that the day when "D" and my father were out evaluating the cotton crops, a widow maker tree limb broke off from a large tree and fell in front of the horse my father was riding on. It caused the horse to go up on his hind legs and my father to fall off and crack open his skull. I chose not to believe any of those rumors that I started to hear when I was around ten years old. It couldn't possibly be true. At that time, I believed he loved my mother and I very much. But thinking back, when I heard that "D" saw to the funeral of my father and that quite soon after that, we were invited to live with him in his Plantation's main home and my mother was invited to share his bed, I started to have some doubts.

The ravaging went on for around six months. I think the only thing that made him stop was that he noticed I was becoming thicker around my belly area and my breasts were becoming larger and firmer. I didn't know what was happening to me as I had only had my menses for around eight months staring when I was twelve. That had stopped coming for the past several months. It wasn't even my mother who noticed and said something to me. It was my Servant Josephine who had tended to me for many years. She said, "My child, you can no longer get into your pantaloons. I know what you eat and you haven't been eating any more than usual." She was fussing about me and said, "Good God child, you are going to have a child of your own?" I was very young and very naïve. She asked me whom I had been having sex with and I told her that I never did have sex with anyone. I loved Josephine and I did trust her. However, I couldn't risk this information getting back to my mother. I needed time to let all of this sink in. What was I going to do? I had no idea what to do. Josephine realized that she was losing the battle of my coming forward with a name but she also cared enough about me and didn't want me to go through this ordeal on my own. She only speculated at that point that I was with child. She knew that my mother's doctor would be coming to see my mother for her weekly visit toward the end of the week and she told me I would need to speak to him about my situation. I realized then just how much Josephine truly loved me. I started to cry and she reached out and held me tight and said, "Don't cry my child, everything is going to be okay. I am here for you." She told me she wouldn't say anything to my parents. She just wanted me to speak with the doctor and have an exam to make sure that I was indeed with child. Unbeknownst to her, I was with "D's" child.

The doctor had me come to his office in town two days

later with Josephine. He did determine that I was pregnant. He demanded to know who the boy was that I had sex with. He wanted to know if it was one of the servants or one of their children or perhaps a boy from the school house down the road? I refused to say a word to him and he said by law, since I was only 14 and still a child, he had to tell my parents. He accompanied myself and Josephine back to the Plantation that afternoon. When 'D', myself, Josephine and the doctor were all standing outside of my mother's room, the doctor said to them, "I have some upsetting news to tell you. Your very young daughter Maria is pregnant." My mother made a small sounding gasp and she started to cry. "D" acted all pious and demanded to know who the young man was that had fathered my child. I looked him straight in the eyes and said, "I don't think you really want me to say his name out loud right here and now do you?" "D" composed himself and quickly said "You are right—this is a family matter and should not be discussed any further in front of the doctor and the help!"

A week later "D" told me he was sending me to New Orleans, Louisiana to have the baby and he said that he was making arrangements for the child to be adopted. I was so young and confused. I couldn't fully comprehend all that was happening to me. I was so sad to be leaving my mother but relieved that I would be able to get away from "D" at least for a few months. Also, I felt relieved that with my being sent away quickly, I would not be around my mother and risk my wanting to tell her who the father of my unborn child actually was. It would have brought on her death that much quicker knowing that I had been ravaged by the man she so deeply loved and appreciated. I thought it would break her heart. The day I left, I went to the outside of my mother's room to say good-bye. She was lying in her bed just staring up at the ceiling. She seemed to have deteriorated so much more even from the day before. I saw tears flowing out from the side of her face. I couldn't kiss her good-bye as coming in close contact with people with Consumption was not advised. I said, "I love you mother and will be back soon so we can sing together again." She whispered, "I am so sorry my precious Maria. Know that I love you very much and am counting the days until your return." I blew her a kiss as Josephine was in the hallway telling me that I must hurry if I was going to catch my train.

OLD URSULINE CONVENT
1749-1753
NEXT TO SITE OF FIRST BUILDING ERECTED IN 1734

HOME OF URSULINE NUNS WHO CAME FROM FRANCE
"TO RELIEVE THE POOR, SICK AND PROVIDE EDUCATION
FOR YOUNG GIRLS"

FIRST GIRLS' SCHOOL IN LOUISIANA
OLDEST BUILDING IN MISSISSIPPI VALLEY

HOUSE OF REPUTE

Josephine, the handler that "D" had hired, and I all went to the train terminal. Josephine hugged me tight and told me not to be sad or worry too much. She told me how much she loved and cared for me and would see me when I returned. She said to the handler, who was named Joseph, "Take good care of my girl and bring her back safely to us." Joseph was hired to be with me all the way to New Orleans where I was to be taken to the Ursuline Convent. The convent was a place where young girls could go to give birth. It was also a place where young girls who were involved in prostitution could go to try and get clean and off of the streets. It was just a loving place where young women in need could be taken care of. It was run by a woman named Sister Veronica.

I had never been away from home before and had no idea what I would have to do at the convent, or how people would react to me. Joseph carried my bag and he hired another man whom we met at the train station to give us a horse and buggy ride to the Usuline Convent. Joseph told me that he would also be coming back in around two to three months to bring me back to the Diamond Dust Plantation.

I was first met at the gate by a woman named Sister Jolynn. She explained to me that she would be taking me to meet Sister Veronica, the head nun at the Ursuline Convent. Sister Jolynn could sense my apprehension and was so sweet to me. She put me at ease and assured me that everything was going to be okay. Sister Jolynn went through a few of the house rules that I would need to abide by, but she did it in such a manner that I didn't feel I was being talked down to. We talked for a few minutes and then Sister Veronica entered the room. I could actually feel her presence. She came to me with an outstretched hand and when I placed my hand in hers, she laid her other hand on top of mine and said, "Welcome to our home Maria, I think you will be a good fit." I was no longer scared. I felt a strange sense of security and peace. I speculated Sister Veronica was in her early fifties and she wasn't what I would call beautiful, but with each passing day, she became more and more beautiful to me. As I got to spend many hours talking with her, I learned that she was of Italian and Irish descent. She also shared that she loved to read. She would read any and all books she could get her hands on. Although she was not formally educated, she was so smart and knew so much from all of the literature and books she was constantly reading.

A week had gone by and I was settling into the every day routine at the Ursuline Convent. I kept up with my studies which were taught by two younger nuns and I kept mostly to myself. I was polite to the other young girls who were in the same predicament as me, but I didn't want to become too friendly with any of them as I never wanted to let my guard down and say anything about who the father of my unborn child was.

In the early mornings, we were all required to go to Mass. We were encouraged to participate in the prayers and the hymns. I knew many of the songs from the years of attending church back in Mississippi and I just let my voice soar. The first time I sang out, I saw the other girls and nuns turn and look at me. I was secure enough in myself to know that they were not looking at me out of curiosity but out of admiration for my voice. I do have to admit I used that opportunity to showcase my gift from God. It was highly inappropriate what happened at the end of what became my solo. They all applauded! It was then that I bonded with all of them. From that moment on, they would have me sing before and after each meal, during evening prayers and of course at Mass. Sister Veronica even allowed us to sit in our social room and just sing popular songs. The other girls just loved those times and I was so happy to see that even the proper nuns were participating. Sister Veronica came to me after the first time I sang at Mass and said, "Maria, I didn't know God was sending us such a special gift. You have the voice of an angel my child."

One night going into the third week of my stay there, Sister Veronica was out in the hallway and heard me crying. I was saying my prayers and asking God how could he have allowed "D" to do what he did to me? She came into my room and comforted me with her soft voice and she stroked the back of my head as my face was buried on her shoulder. She asked me if the "D" I was referring to was my stepfather?

I whispered, "Yes."

"My child you are so strong and don't ever let anyone else tell you otherwise," she said. "If you want me to keep the secret of what I just heard you tell the Lord, I will. It can be just between you and I and our heavenly father."

What I didn't know that night was that Sister Veronica had no intentions of ever sending me back to Mississippi where the monster "D" lived and would be waiting for me to come back to him. Sister Veronica did not take kindly to young girls being ravaged.

After I gave birth to my son, he was taken from my arms by the midwife who worked at the convent. I remember that the pain of giving up my son was just as unbearable as my ravagings and I had to use my frozen ritual to get me through. I realistically knew that I couldn't possibly care for a child when I was practically a child myself but I didn't want to let him go. I never even allowed myself the right to name him. He would have been too real to me then and I couldn't bear it.

Around a month passed by and I physically healed from childbirth. Sister Veronica came to me with a proposal.

"Child, I can make it so you never have to go back to the life you came from. It may not be a wonderful life I am offering you, but I can offer you a safe home to live in where you will not be ravaged by men and I will have a way to keep my eyes and ears on you. It would mean you wouldn't be able to communicate with your mother and you cannot get word back to anyone in Mississippi that I am offering to give you a start at a new life. It would have to be our secret."

COURTESAN COTTAGE

Sister Veronica told me that I had to decide quickly exactly what I was going to do. I needed guidance so I went to St. Louis Cathedral and said a prayer. I walked out of the church and through Jackson Square. I stood in the middle of it and looked up to the sky. I said to myself that I would spin around seven times and open my eyes. Depending on the direction I would be facing when I opened my eyes, that would determine my destiny. If I wound up facing the Mississippi River, it was a sign from God that I was to return to my mother and the ravaging of "D", I would be going back. But if I wound up facing any of the other three streets, it was meant to be that I would be going in a different direction with my life—I would be moving forward. I couldn't help but feel anxious about what was to be my destiny, my destination. I did as I had planned and spun around seven times. I was a bit dizzy when I opened my eyes. It was the most pivotal moment of my life. I started to walk forward and forbade myself from looking back as that might cause me to re-negotiate the promise I had just made to myself. From that moment on the child Maria Pierre Quinones was gone and the young woman "Pierre" had emerged. I looked around my surroundings and the first thing I set my sight on was the St. Louis Cathedral. It looked so hauntingly beautiful and it offered me so much comfort in my time of need. From that day forward, I would never use my real first or last name. I simply became Pierre Louis.

Sister Veronica couldn't risk walking me to the train station in case anyone were to have seen us together and would have said something to the police. That was, of course, assuming "D" would even report my disappearance to anyone. She chose All Saints' Day for my departure as the city was full of people in masks to playfully disguise who they really were. Many women were beautifully dressed in gowns and the men were in black tie attire. They were going to different balls and parties. She felt I would be less noticed or remembered on this particular evening in my very simple dress and mask. Sister Veronica's plan was to give me a day to get to my new destination. Then the next day when Joseph would arrive to take me back home, she would take him up to my room and they would both see that my room was all tidy and clean but that I was not there nor were all of my belongings. She would guide Joseph into thinking the only logical conclusion—I had run away. Sister Veronica was prepared to deal with any and all backlash that would come with her so irresponsibly allowing such a thing to happen.

I was discretely led out to the side of the Ursuline Convent by Sister Jolynn. She was dressed in regular street clothes, not her habit. Sister Veronica was there and hugged me and said, "Child the loving arms of God will protect you in my absence. You have become a daughter to me and I will keep track of you through my associates. I know you are going on to be a blessed young woman and never look back on the past. You are to move forward and know that there is someone who loves you deeply and I will keep you in my thoughts and prayers. We are forever connected."

She looked up to the sky which was illuminated by a beautiful full moon. She took my hand to her heart and said, "Whenever you look up and see the lace around the moon, know that our hearts will be together soon."

I thought those were the most beautiful words I ever heard. Those very words stayed with me and haunted me for quite a long time. I knew I would have to do something with them someday—I just didn't know when or how.

Another nun and Sister Jolynn walked me to the block before the train station. She hugged me too and gave me a little medallion of the patron saint of their order—Saint Ursula, who is the patron saint of school girls. She said to me, "Godspeed Pierre—Essayons." I asked her what that word meant and she said it is French for, "We will try." I remember thinking that trying is exactly what I must do. I must try and get through this venture of getting on with my life.

Sister Veronica had instructed me to get off at the first train stop and to walk around and get lost in the crowd. I was to pretend that I had to get off as I had an accident in my undergarments and needed my bag from the conductor so I could change my soiled under clothing. After I had my bag, I quickly followed the crowds who were heading towards what I assumed was the French Quarter (Vieux Carré). There were so many people!

There was such excitement in the air and there was such a hustle and bustle going on like I had never experienced. I remembered thinking I wished I could have been part of the party atmosphere, but knew that now was not the time for joyous festivities. I was on a different path now, but thought that perhaps someday I would experience those wonderful city experiences. I walked around just getting a feel for things as I had around 30 minutes to wait before I would encounter the two women Sister Veronica told me I was to meet. I noticed that several of the women were stylishly dressed. If they were not wearing a party gown, they had on the popular outfit which was that of a skirt which had drapes, folds and pleats and some of them were bustled. The purpose of the bustle was to expand the fullness of the back of the skirt or dress. The top part of their outfits were Basques, which were long, jacket-like fitted bodices. Some ladies were even wearing hobble-skirts. They were called that due to how tight and form fitting they were. It seemed that many of the clothes they were wearing were made out of velvet. I was in awe of the beauty and sophistication of these women. I felt like such a child in their presence. I was so caught between being a child and a woman at that point in my life. I dug deep within myself and stood up straight and held my head high. Someday I was going to be just as beautifully dressed and proud as these women seemed to be. I just needed to come into my own.

After 30 minutes went by, I went to the General Store in the area and I looked around and started to get very nervous. What if the women didn't meet me? Where would I go? I had some money on me and my jewels from "D," but I didn't know how to turn those in for cash. I started to panic when I heard a beautiful sing song voice say, "Darling, are you looking for us?" It was a very pretty young woman with auburn brown hair and another just as pretty with dark, almost black hair. These women were so elegant and beautifully coifed. They were wearing the latest fashions and smelled of the finest perfumes. I knew what they did for a living as Sister Veronica explained to me where I would be going and staying. From what I had heard growing up, I thought that prostitutes were dirty and downtrodden. Not these two ladies. They introduced themselves to me. The first one was named Dee and the other woman was named Irene. They were polite but not overly friendly. They told me that they would be taking me to a place called "Courtesan Cottage." I later learned that Courtesan is a euphemism to designate a comforter, escort, mistress or a prostitute especially one of dignified etiquette. We walked for around ten minutes with the two of them leading the way and me scurrying behind them carrying my bag. When we arrived, I was quite surprised by how small of a building it was. But then again, it truly was a cottage. It wasn't actually a brothel as the women who lived there did not provide their services at the cottage. I remember thinking how could someplace so small house women who provide unethical services for men. To me, these women seemed larger than life! I was fascinated and captivated by them. The interesting thing about the cottage was that it was just the place where four ladies lived but did not practice their trade. The cottage was behind the "French House" located on 213-215 Basin Street. The French House was run by Madam Frances Mantley. The ladies of the house were known for miming a certain act using their thumbs to entice visitors. I was led past the house and right to the cottage. My chaperones told me to just keep my head down and go past the ladies who were situated on the veranda.

"Don't pay no attention to them now, there will be plenty of time for you to meet all of those ladies," Irene said. "But for right now we need for you to meet Miss Margaret, the lady of the house."

I didn't know what to expect of Miss Margaret but I was pleasantly surprised when Irene introduced me to her. She was an attractive woman in her mid forties. She had red hair and I could see her Irish heritage shining through in her fair white skin. She was properly dressed and had a twinkle in her eye. She said, "Welcome to my home Pierre, I think you will be a good fit."

There were four women who lived with Miss Margaret in her little cottage. She wasn't exactly the madam of the house but she was somewhat of a talent agent. I eventually learned that she set up "appointments" for these women. Miss Margaret was a savvy businesswoman. She advertised her beautiful and special ladies in the local Mascot Publication's Society Column and said they were simply, "Available for Companion Services." These women would go to the theatre or to lavish balls with men who were visiting from out of town. The men were very wealthy and affluent, as the price that Miss Margaret could charge required a large billfold. Then whatever was negotiated between the women and these gents after hours was on their own time and dime. Miss Margaret turned her eyes to the disreputable part of the business but still let her purse be filled with coins she collected from the ladies as was their arrangement. Miss Margaret set up the dates for the ladies and the ladies paid her a negotiated percentage to keep a roof over them, keep them safe and provide them with their livelihood. Miss Margaret felt she was a very religious woman. She was able to convince herself that since she did not actually reap any rewards from the things these women were doing after the first part of the dates, I assumed she didn't feel she was actually committing any sins or at least that is what she told God and how she worked this out all in her mind and her soul. She believed she was not doing anything wrong. I remember thinking it is funny how we all tell ourselves little lies to get by.

When I agreed to Sister Veronica's proposal of going to live at Courtesan Cottage, I knew I too was going to have to be providing a service. Fortunately for me, it had nothing to do with my using my body to service men. I was going to be using my voice to entice men to come into establishments where there would be women there using their bodies to service men. What I was hired to do was to sing in different brothels and pleasure palaces. Miss Margaret laid out the rules for me. I was also expected to clean, do some of the cooking and help with the washing of the clothes around the cottage. These were all tasks that were new to me as when I was living back home on "D's" Plantation, I had servants to tend to all of my needs.

Now I was doing the tending and although I wouldn't say I enjoyed it, I felt freer than I had ever felt in my life. I was beholden to no man. It took a while but I was slowly getting over my fear of "D" finding me or another man taking advantage of me. The ladies in the Courtesan Cottage provided me with a security I had not had for quite some time in my life. It took me a month to get a feel for things around the cottage and for the women living under the roof. I got to know them each personally by having conversations with them and found out what their "specialties" were. They called Dee—"Dicey Dee." I learned that her talent was that she was a phenomenal card hustler and gambler. Men would hire her to go along with them to the gambling saloons and play along as a dimwit and then she would take the unsuspecting participants for their coins. She also had been known as a risk taker in the boudoir. Certain men sought her out for her willingness to do just about anything—certainly the things their wives at home were not willing to do.

Irene was the classiest of all the ladies in Miss Margaret's house. She had gone to a fine women's school and was very polished and poised. But how she appeared in the formal settings she was hired to accompany men to, was a far cry from how she was when she was alone in private with them. It was like she wore two faces – prim and proper and then anything but. She also would always keep her fashion boots on during any and all of her dates. She became known as "Knock-in Boots Irene."

There were two other women who lived in the cottage. One was Holly. She was known as "Handy Holly." Her regular talents were that of a seamstress. After I started making money singing at the different saloons and brothels, I would have her make me beautiful dresses. They were not made of high-quality fabrics, but she did a beautiful job with the designs. She received her nickname for how nimble her hands and fingers were in all aspects of her life. She was an excellent seamstress and several of the women's clothing shops in town hired her to make beautiful outfits for the upper echelon ladies of society. She could sew together a beautiful dress and top coat in a couple of days. And what she was able to do for men with her hands became her special talent—she only used her hands.

The fourth woman who lived in the cottage was named Erina. Her name was Celtic Gaelic meaning Ireland. Her heart truly was as big as Ireland. Erina was sought out for her ability to comfort anyone who came to her with either physical or emotional traumas. Within her mere presence, you felt an overwhelming sense of serenity. She was a tall blonde woman with a dazzling smile. It wasn't so much her beauty, which she was gifted with, but her voice and her mannerisms just put you at ease. She would touch your hand or shoulder and you felt a flow of comfort coming from her. She dabbled a little bit in voodoo, but she also had a medical background having worked with her father for many years who was a physician's assistant of sorts to the prostitutes on the streets of New Orleans. Her father and her did not judge the girls, but offered them medical services after poorly performed procedures were done to them or when they needed medicine to help with the symptoms of venereal disease which was rampant. Erina simply became known as the "Healer." Men would say that she had the power to heal their afflictions and she could make them rise to the occasion. I never asked her or any of the other ladies why they went into the profession they had chosen. That was their business and not mine. I assumed they must have had their reasons as I too had my reasons for doing what I was doing. Sometimes circumstances take over and dictate our life choices.

For the next few years, I would sing a couple times a week at the French House and just a few other saloons near the cottage. Usually these establishments would just have a piano player called "professors" playing popular piano tunes. I would just accompany them and sing for the customers.   I was too young to be working in the more popular pleasure clubs and brothels. Miss Margaret didn't want to attract the attention of the local police department or the church-going members of the community who would have frowned on a child being exploited in these sin-filled establishments. I couldn't believe how quickly the time had gone by since I first arrived in New Orleans. I was getting along well with the ladies at the Courtesan Cottage. We had bonded together in a family like way. We looked out for one another. Since I was getting older, it was decided that my singing career would start to take off. One afternoon, before I was going to go over to the French House, Miss Margaret sat me down for a little talk.

"Pierre, within the next couple of days you are going to be meeting a very powerful man who is going to decide if he is going to, "take you under his wing," she said. "If he likes what he hears, he has said he would be willing to further your singing career. If this indeed does happen for you, the responsibilities I originally assigned to you around the cottage will no longer be yours."

I remember I went to sleep that night and thanked God for this possibility. I have to be honest and say I liked the idea of not having to clean up after, launder the clothes or cook for the "CC's" anymore. "CC's was the affectionate name I gave to them collectively. They were the Courtesan Cottage Clandestines. Even at this point in my life I was making enough money that I could have moved out and had my own room somewhere in town, but I felt safe in Miss Margaret's home and I cherished the friendship of the CC's. Although they were not actually blood to me, they were the closest thing I had to that.

I had heard through Sister Veronica that my mother did pass. I knew there was not any possibility of my going back to Mississippi to pay my respects. I did that privately at St. Louis Cathedral. The cathedral had become my safe haven when I needed shelter or to be close to God. I went there and lit a candle to my mother's memory and thanked God that she found peace from her physical suffering. I also said a quick prayer for myself and thanked him for having me be safe and looked out after by the CC's and Miss Margaret. As it turned out, Miss Margaret was actually Sister Veronica's sister. Although the two sisters had both chosen somewhat different paths in life – I thought that there was not much difference between a whore house and a convent—one tends to the needs of the body and the other to the needs of the soul.

THICK LEGGED WOMAN

At 18 I started coming into my own. As a child and teenager, I was pretty enough but always more on the heavy, voluptuous side. I was thick. But a lot of men seemed to like that, especially when I started out singing in the different saloons and eventually in brothels. They said I was something they could sink their teeth into. A lot of them got the wrong idea about me because of the places I was singing at. Just because I was working in whore houses didn't mean I was a whore. I was there to be the entertainment but not necessarily the entertainment they were there for. I was there to wet their appetites—I was the first course. I was very apprehensive about entering into this line of work. I had no idea what to expect or how the crowds would accept me, or more importantly, my voice. I had put together a routine that had to be run by the very powerful man Miss Margaret told me about. This powerful man was Mr. Tim Anderson. He requested that my routine or what he was calling, "my showcase," be presented to him using local band members that he had handpicked. Miss Margaret took me to a local pleasure club one evening and I was introduced to the band members. They were all older than me. Some of them were actually into their 30's and 40's. After I asked them to play, "We Sat Beneath the Maple on the Hill," by Gussie Lord Davis without my singing the first time, I knew why these special men were chosen. They were outstanding and mesmerizing. After I got a feel for their style, I then joined in singing on the second take of the song. Besides Miss Margaret, there were only a few people in the back room of the building, but I would definitely say we shook the rafters. It was like we had been playing together for years. The band leader was named Jacob. When we finished the first song, he said, "Miss Pierre, I believe you are going to be a good fit." We rehearsed several songs that evening and when we were done, Jacob came over to me with a bottle of dark liquid and two glasses. He poured us each two inches into our glasses and he said, "Here's to working with such a wonderful, young and talented lady." I had never had a drink of alcohol other than on the Holidays with my mother. I took a sip so as to not be disrespectful. I actually stared coughing and tears flowed down my face from the burn. He laughed and said "Laissez les bons temps rouler - let the good times roll!"

After we finished rehearsing that night, I was surprised to see that Miss Margaret had left. I was planning on walking back to the cottage when I was approached by a man who I speculated was in his early 30's. He extended his hand out to mine for a handshake. I accepted his hand and thought how hard and rough his hands were. He said, "Good evening ma'am, my name is Frankie. I will be escorting you home tonight." I was taken aback by how he called me ma'am. Keep in mind, I never let anyone know my age except for the women at the Courtesan Cottage, Sister Veronica and Miss Margaret. I certainly did not look young. I looked more like a 25-year-old woman but still I never thought of myself as being a ma'am. I asked him who decided that? I was a bit apprehensive about being in the presence of a man who I did not know as I was still somewhat leery of men. He said, "That has been decided by Mr. Anderson and what Mr. Anderson says—goes." He apologized if he was curt or abrupt in his introduction, but he assured me it was in my best interest to let him provide this service. The manager of the pleasure club, whose name was Kenneth, came over to me as he saw that I was not comfortable with this situation. He assured me that this man was legitimate and did indeed work for Mr. Anderson. Since it was getting late and I was exhausted, I didn't see the point in putting up a fight. Frankie went and got my shawl for me and he allowed me a few minutes to say good-bye to my new band members.

On that first night's walk home, we didn't even speak.

It was just so odd and uncomfortable and I didn't feel like making small talk with a total stranger. When we arrived at my front door, he just tipped his hat and said, "I will be seeing you tomorrow evening Miss Pierre. I will be here promptly at 6:30. Good night." I politely nodded and said "The same to you Frankie."

My head was reeling from excitement and apprehension from the night's unfolding. I realized I had to get more comfortable and familiar with my band members. That first night I did not show off in anyway. I kept it simple but let it come through in my voice and my demeanor that I was a competent, confident singer. I decided the next night, I would show them what I was really capable of. Sure enough, Frankie came back the next evening at exactly 6:30. He tipped his hat and said, "Good evening Miss Pierre, shall we be on our way?" After that first night, Miss Margaret explained to me that she would not to be the one to escort me to Mr. Anderson's pleasure club, it would be Frankie who would be looking out for me from then on.

After the second, third and fourth night of rehearsals, I was becoming more and more confident in myself and my stage presence. On the fifth night of rehearsals, when Frankie came to escort me, he actually did a double take. For the first four evenings I wore clean, proper and stylish skirts and jackets. However, that fifth night, I wore a form fitting long green dress that I borrowed from Holly's clos-et. I had my hair put up in a bun with an angel trumpet flower delicately placed in my up-do.

That evening there were a few more people at our re-hearsal that I didn't recognize. But I welcomed having more of an audience so that I could get comfortable using the proper theatrics to accompany my singing and they would be the ones to get the first glimpse of what my stage show would encompass. Perhaps they could offer myself and the band some feedback. I couldn't believe how I was not at all nervous or apprehensive about performing in front of these strangers. I felt like it was just part of who I was and I just felt so blessed to be able to share my voice with others.   That evening I asked Jacob if I could start out with a popular New Orleans song that started out with a very slow, engaging vibe that showcased all the notes I could hit. Jazz music had not yet been specifically defined, but this song had the earthy characteristics and the soul-fullness of a new, upcoming music genre, called Ragtime. One of the band members played the comet which was an instrument similar to the trumpet and with that sound, the piano man and my voice, I felt we were captivating to the ear. I just felt it. We were on to something. The band members and I were connecting and we were connecting to the people in our small audience. There was one man in the audience who just sat there staring at me. It felt like his eyes were penetrating my soul but it wasn't an alarming feeling but rather a feeling of my wanting to bring him into my presence. I gave my heart, soul and voice that night. I was flawless and so was our band. I went over to talk to Jacob about what our next set should be like. He seemed a bit flustered and ill at ease.

"Jacob is everything okay, am I doing justice to the band with my singing?" I asked.

"Pierre, you are outstanding tonight. You are hitting every note and you are doing more than justice to our repertoire, but I don't think you know who that is in the audience—the man who is staring at you?"

I told him that no, I had no idea who that gentleman was. He said, "You had better get to know the players in this town Pierre—that is Mr. Tim C. Anderson."

I told myself not to get nervous or act any differently. I needed to keep on singing and belting out my next set just as I had done with the first two. When we were wrapping up for the night, Kenneth asked me to join him at a table off to the side. Since Frankie was not yet there to escort me back home, I said that I would. I went and sat down at the table that already had been preset with a bottle of whiskey and two glasses. I was waiting for Kenneth to say something as we were both just sitting there. He saw Mr. Anderson approaching us. He quickly got up from his seat and said, "Pierre, I would like to introduce you to Mr. Anderson." I did a polite nod and he extended his hand out for a handshake. I did the same and he took my hand to his lips and kissed my hand. No man had ever done that to me before. I felt a strange flush go through my body. We sat down and Kenneth poured us both a drink from the bottle. Mr. Anderson lifted his glass and he clicked my drink and said, "Pierre, I will take you on." I took a sip of the whiskey and looked him directly in the eyes. I wasn't quite sure what to say or if I should say anything at all. I didn't know exactly what he meant by his statement, but before I could gather my thoughts and utter any words, he again extended his hand for mine and again kissed my shaking hand. What ran through my mind was if I would have to do Mr. Anderson a service for him taking me on? I started to sputter out something and before I could formulate my words, he left the room.

When I arrived back at the cottage that night after Frankie had dropped me off, only Erina and Dee were home. It was their evening off and they were just staying in getting their wardrobes coordinated for their next evening's outings. I asked them if they could tell me anything they knew about Mr. Anderson. They filled me in on everything I probably didn't want to know. They had heard that at a young age he had started out as a hustler working both with the police and against them in the same transaction. He at times went to the demimonde side – the half world. He would portray himself as a politician, a pillar of society but would dabble in and derive profit from drugs and gambling and his favorite vice—sexual promiscuity. They had heard about him and his tastes, and I started to worry that I might be his next treat. Why else would he be doing all of this for me? I couldn't let these thoughts and worries interfere with my upcoming debut at his other more reputable pleasure club than the one that I had been rehearsing at. The band and I rehearsed for two more nights and we all felt we were ready. The only thing we were lacking was a name for our band. I always liked how people from New Orleans would say, "Hey, can you throw in a lagniappe into that bag of potatoes, or could I have a dozen rolls with a lagniappe?" Lagniappe means just a little something extra. At the last night's rehearsal, I ran the idea by the band. They were thrilled with it and that is how "Pierre and the Lagniappe Orchestra" came to fruition. We would be taking four days off before we were scheduled to do our first performance. It gave us all time to get physically and emotionally prepared. It was during this downtime that a box arrived from a local storekeeper. Inside was a beautiful green dress. There was a note that simply read, "You are to wear this dress when you perform for the first time at my pleasure club. In exchange for this opportunity I am providing you, you are to be available to me when I want to hear an angel sing." Also, in the box with the dress was a little black satchel. In it were three strands of glass beads – one purple, one green and one gold. Again, I still didn't know what he was expecting from me, but it was the first time I was given a beautiful necklace where I hadn't had to be ravaged for the gift.   From that day forward, once a year on the anniversary of our first meeting, I would receive a beautiful green dress with a card that simply read: "From TCA—looking forward to seeing my angel in green." I always assumed he liked the color green due to his Irish heritage, but perhaps it was because it brought out the emerald color of my eyes. It was strange to be in a platonic relationship with this man who was so powerful and respected by many. But here were also a lot of people who did not like him for all of the things he was involved in that were on the wrong side of the law and morality. He was both feared and revered.

It was an exciting time for me. I was busy tending to last minute touches for myself for my big night and went into town. There were signs up about myself and our band and where we would be performing in two days! It was in-credulous to see my own name on paper and plastered on different windows of the shops around town. I had never felt such a feeling of pride. I reflected on how far I had come in the few years since giving up my son and moving into the Courtesan Cottage. I realized I was blessed and I started to cry on my walk back home. They were not tears of sadness, but of contentment and exhilaration.

Of course, Frankie was there to pick me up right on time. This time when he saw me, he said, "I apologize for staring at you Miss Pierre, it is just that you look so beautiful tonight."

I actually felt sorry for him because he was so nervous about even talking to me. "Frankie, thank you for the compliment and for taking good care of me in getting me to and from my rehearsals and now to my big night," I said. "I am glad you are here with me."

I could see a contained smile on his face and a slight blush on his face. He tipped his hat to me and said, "Miss Pierre, please believe me when I say the pleasure is all mine."

We were off and both of us had a little spring in our steps. When I arrived at the pleasure club, I was taken through the back door. They didn't want us to be visible to the many people who had already gathered to see us until the curtain came up. I did a little bit of vocal stretching and the band was tuning up. Jacob and the band members complimented me on how lovely I looked especially in the beautiful green dress. They also said that the beautiful beaded necklace I had on was spectacular. I couldn't help but run my fingers over all of the beads and appreciate where they came from. Thirty minutes later we heard all of the voices in the club area growing louder with anticipation. The curtain was finally raised and we performed three sets. There was a table for one, off to the right side where TCA was seated. He stared at me throughout the entire show and didn't leave his seat, not even when we took our breaks. He didn't ask to speak to me that night but when we were finishing up our final song, I saw him stand and rise. He tipped his hat to me and I saw a glistening from under his eyes. I had moved him to tears. And then he was gone. All of the important people in my life were there with me to celebrate that night—Miss Margaret, Irene, Erina, Holly and Dee. They all hugged and kissed me and congratulated me on my success that evening. There was also another woman with them that I thought I recognized but I couldn't put it all together. That was until that woman came up to me and hugged me and said, "My child, you have made me so proud."

I had felt that embrace before and felt the comfort of those arms and voice. It was Sister Veronica! She was dressed in regular clothing. I couldn't believe she was actually here. That made the entire night and experience all the more special. It was getting very late and I had a bit too much to drink. I knew it was time to go when Frankie who had been patiently sitting at a table with some of the band members came to me and said, "Miss Pierre, are you ready to go?"

I didn't want the night to end but I too knew it was

time. I was a bit unsteady on my feet. That is when Frank-ie said, "Miss Pierre, could I have the pleasure of guid-ing you home?" Before I could answer, he slid his arm through mine and made sure he had a good hold on me so I wouldn't fall. That simple gesture allowed me to leave my big night without making a fool of myself. Frankie was becoming my protector. He saw me to the front door. Miss Margaret and the other ladies had gone home ahead of me and were waiting for me when I arrived. Frankie turned me over to them and they helped get me to my room and undressed. I lied in my bed and just kept on re-living the entire night over and over in my mind. I didn't feel like I had become a star—but rather a very bright moonbeam. I was really beginning to shine.

CHER AMI

I came up for air in telling Mr. Baynes my story of when I was younger and first went to live in New Orleans. I couldn't believe how quickly five hours went by that first day! I was exhausted and the bottle of whiskey was dry. We decided to take two days off before meeting again. I needed to finally get through all of my mail and go and see the attorney who had written me the large check before cashing it. I also needed to do some financial planning as now it seemed as though I was going to be having some reoccurring income coming in from *Lace Around the Moon*. I also needed to get myself together and figure out how I was going to start the process of finding my son.

Two days later when I met Mr. Baynes on the same park bench in Jackson Square, I felt like it was becoming therapeutic for me to be doing this. I felt like I was taking this burden I had been carrying around off of my soul. Of course, we started off with a drink, and I again closed my eyes, starting up again where I had left off...

From the first time I had performed at TCA's pleasure

club through the next many years, I was performing at least six times a week with our band. Then around five years into what was known as Storyville, TCA had me singing at Mahogany Hall, the most beautiful brothel in Storyville. The Madam of that House was Miss Lala White. Storyville was the red-light district of New Orleans that started up in 1897 and went all the way through 1917. It was established by the City Council to regulate prostitution and drugs. It designated thirty-eight blocks of town as the area where prostitution was tolerated and regulated although it was still illegal. This part of our town was nicknamed the District, the "Tenderloin District" and TCA was becoming known as the unofficial Mayor of Storyville.

As Storyville was quite a bit further of a distance for me to travel to in order to get to all of my shows, I reluctantly moved into a little shotgun house that I was able to afford on my own closer to the District. Irene moved in with me as she was offered a job at Miss Lala's House. My other CC's—Holly and Erina wanted to stay with Miss Margaret and not get involved with Storyville employment. They were doing very well financially working for Miss Margaret. Dee was the first of the CC's to leave the profession. She had met a young architect and she told us she was going to be "getting out of the life." This young man's name was Michael McNally. He obviously knew what Dee did for a living, but he wanted to put that behind them and start off fresh. He built them a beautiful home outside of the Quarter less than ten miles away. It was in Metairie which was just starting to become urbanized as prior to that time, most of its citizens were sharecroppers. Michael was credited with turning Metairie into a place where families would want to come to live. He wanted Dee and himself to become contributing members of this new community and he never wanted Dee to again be referred to as "Dicey Dee." He actually started calling her Deanna which was her birth name and they went on to be very happy together.

Over the next period of my life, Frankie became more and more of my protector. He would come and escort me to each of my performances from my new house which was around 8 blocks from Basin Street where Storyville was thriving. Things were definitely much rougher in this section of town but I always felt safe with Frankie looking out after me and with Irene living with me. It was known around town that I was an employee of TCA and no one wanted to say or do anything improper to me as that would mean they would have to deal with Frankie and more importantly, TCA. No one wanted to mess with him or be on his bad side. He was just too powerful and he had the ability to have his problems eliminated. It was understood that I was TCA's possession of sorts. I knew TCA was looking out for my well being but sometimes

I got the feeling he simply didn't want any other man to have access to me. For all the years that I had been working for TCA, he never once expected anything from me. I think I did for his soul what the other women were doing for his body—especially Miss White.

I was very comfortable with Frankie over the next several years. I knew that his job was to make sure that I was safe, but I also felt he was there to keep an eye on me so that I wouldn't develop a relationship with a man. I never once tested the waters of seeing what would happen if I did have a male suitor or admirer. However, I was getting older but I was still a young healthy woman with natural needs and I started to think of romance and more importantly, companionship. I eventually opened up to Frankie all about "D" and what he had done to me. I also told him my entire life story and about my son. I actually saw a few tears escape from Frankie's eyes when I was telling him my story. He never wiped the tears away as that would have meant that I knew he had cried. After that night, we never again spoke about it. I knew that Frankie had feelings for me and he thought of himself as my knight in shining armor. But I also had a feeling he may have even deeper feelings for me, but he was never anything other than respectful to me. I was so glad to have him in my life. He was the brother I never had. Frankie also told me about his life growing up. He was from a very large Irish

Catholic family and was very close to his siblings. Their surname was Quigley and they were all proud of their Irish heritage. He was a very hard-working man who also did roofing as a side business. I thought to myself that was why his hands were so hard and rough. I learned he was in his late twenties and had different women in his life but none that he had ever wanted to settle down with or start a family with. I got to know Frankie during those many years with the arrangement of him as my escort. But I do have to say that I learned he had a dark edge to him. I never thought Frankie was anything other than a gentleman until one night when there was a man at TCA's establishment who had gotten heavily intoxicated and made a rude remark to me and went to grab my ample backside. Frankie took out what looked to be like a hammer and brought the full force of the tool down on the man's arm and broke it. I then knew, for sure, that Frankie was the hired muscle.

I lasted at Miss White's for a short period of time. She politely let me go as I had learned she was not comfortable with TCA's attention or relationship with me. I was hired the very next day to work down the street at the Maison de Pierre which was run by Madam Gratia. It was almost as beautiful as Lala White's Mahogany Hall but it had more of a feeling of friendship with the girls in this house than at Mahogany Hall. Madam Gratia was very good to all of her girls and to me. I was making money; a substantial amount of money and I was putting it away so that I could one day afford to buy the Courtesan Cottage. I knew that eventually Miss Margaret had planned to move away from the Quarter and I had actually talked to her about my buying it from her. She had promised before she ever sold it, she would let me make an offer.

Things were uneventful for the next several years. There was harmony in most of the houses. That was until one day when Erina told us about a situation that happened at one of the houses. Word travels fast amongst the girls in the Quarter and in Storyville. It was somewhat of a sisterhood, and although the girls would sometimes fight with each other for better patrons and there was, of course, the jealousy of position and power in the houses, these women were all connected through their situations. And these women would talk. Erina went on to tell us that there was a young woman who had some girls from her house come to her for some medicine for the beating and tearing she took from a client. Erina mentioned that she thought I had met this young-looking girl before at the French House. She actually was friends with Irene. She was just a little thing with dark hair. Erina told me that a patch of it had been pulled out and her face was all bruised and swollen. What had been done to her private parts was even more horrific. These were not uncommon occurrences that happened to the girls by abusive clients, but what the man did after her beating was what captured my attention. The girl said when he was done, he went into his bag and brought out a beautiful necklace and put it around her neck on her battered body. I asked Erina to please let me know where this girl was staying so I could go and find her. I had to find out what this man looked like and any information I could get on him. I thought what were the chances that there could be two men in this world who would ravage you and then be-jewel you with a beautiful necklace? Erina told me the girl's name was "Little Maggie." What the men liked about her was that she was so young looking and petite. She looked to be around 12 or 13 years old. A day later, Erina got word back to me that Little Maggie who was nicknamed Li'l M, said I could come and talk to her. When I arrived, she was lying in a bed and had bandages all over her arms, legs and scalp and she was wearing a beautiful necklace. The scene was so odd in that she was all battered and bruised but wearing a large necklace around her dainty neck. She told me about how this man raped and beat her and then wanted her to have this beautiful diamond and gold neck-lace—he wanted her to wear it. When she told him she couldn't even put it on because of the damage he had done to her body, he lifted up her neck and put it on her. He then cleaned himself up and left. She didn't scream out until after he left because she feared he would kill her right there and then. Also, she wanted to make sure that no one would take the necklace off of her. At that point she didn't know if the jewels were real or not but she wasn't willing to take the chance of it being taken away from her. She said that she was entitled to the necklace for what she was forced to endure. She felt she had earned it. I asked Li'l M what this man looked like and she said he was tall and well built and wore finely tailored clothes and shoes. She said she could smell the money on him. She went on to say he had dark hair and that he smelled very nice. He asked her what her name was and she told him, "Maggie." Li'l M started to cry and tremble a bit and said, "During the rape, he called me Maria over and over again." She said that he didn't beat her until after he again asked her what her name was and she again said, "Maggie." The man said, "No! Your name is Maria!" I felt so sorry for this girl. It was going to be quite some time before she healed from her physical wounds and emotional scars. Erina told me that she was being kicked out of the house where she was working because she could no longer earn her keep. I asked Li'l M if she would want to come and live in my little house with myself and Irene? She started to cry and said that she didn't understand my kindness. I told her I had an extra room and that she could get herself all healed up and then we would talk about things after that. I figured it would be a month or two before she could walk again. She was going to need tending to. I told her I would have to talk to Irene to see if she would be willing to also help out her friend by taking care of her meals. I also told her I would have to make sure Erina would be willing to come over every few days and look in on her, bathe her and dress her wounds. I had no doubts that Irene and Erina would be willing to help Li'l M out. Like I said before, these women were like sisters. I never explained to Li'l M why I took her in. I was positive that it was "D" who did this to her. I never told anyone why except Frankie. That evening when Frankie came to escort me to Maison de Pierre, he could tell there was something amiss. I went on to tell him about what had happened to Li'l M and how I knew it was "D" who did this to her. Why else would he call her Maria and put a necklace on her if it wasn't in fact "D?" I told Frankie that I felt responsible for what had happened to Li'l M and by having her come and live with me until she was back on her feet, that would be my way of making it up to her. If it weren't for myself not going back to Mississippi and the Diamond Dust Plantation, I speculated this would never have happened to Li'l M. I felt I owed her.

REAP WHAT YOU SOW

So now there was myself, Irene and Li'l M all living in my little house. Li'l M was getting stronger by the day. Her hair started to grow back in and her body was healing. However, she was never going to be able to walk again without a limp. After she was able to finally leave the house, I went with her to a small fine jewelry shop back in the Quarter. The Jewelry Store owner did confirm that the necklace was in fact made of genuine diamonds and gold. He estimated it to be worth around $7,000! Li'l M actually started to hyperventilate. She couldn't believe that she may actually have $7,000 to her name. She knew she would need to find someone to buy it from her as she did not want it around reminding her of what had happened to her or take the chance it could possibly be stolen.

That afternoon, Li'l M and I went to St. Louis Cathedral and said a little prayer. We then went out to Jackson Square and sat down for a talk. Li'l M was nervous and said, "I know I have been staying with you for quite sometime, Miss Pierre, and I really appreciate it more than you will ever know. Please give me a little more time before you ask me to leave. I am just not ready to have to go back to my life."

This girl's pleading reminded me so much of myself years earlier where I too was not ready to go back to the life I had that was destroyed by "D." I remembered thinking I was making good money but it was quite a bit to feed and take care of Li'l M financially. I asked her if there was one thing she could do if she didn't have to make a living as a prostitute, what would that be? She told me her dream was always to play the piano. I asked her if she knew how to play and she said that she did and that she was actually pretty good. She would sometimes play at the houses she was working at.

I started to think all of this through and I said, "Li'l M I have a proposition for you. It is going to have to involve you spending some of the money you will make off of the sale of the necklace."

She looked at me inquisitively and said she would gladly part with some of that money if it meant she could stay living with me and not being on her back. I told Li'l M that she would need to buy a used piano and her and I would rent a little store front area in the heart of the French Quarter where many affluent families with children lived. She and I would become business partners. She would teach piano and I would teach singing lessons. I didn't have nearly enough money to open up my own little business but I decided that the next day, I would take the necklaces that "D" had given me, back to the same jeweler and find out their worth. I had no doubt they were authentic jewels, but I obviously needed to know that for a fact. I knew it was going to cost quite a bit of money to start up our little legitimate venture. I also realized I would need to clear this through TCA as I had been working exclusively for him all of these years. I didn't want him to think that I would not still fulfill my singing obligations that he had set up for me. It was just that I wanted to have a little something for myself outside of singing at his clubs and brothels. I wanted to be a businesswoman and with the way things were working out with my meeting Li'l M, I felt it was a sign. How ironic it was that both her and I were ravaged by "D" and by chance, we were talking of having our own little business together. I felt it was fate. Maybe something good could come out of the tragedies that happened to both of us by the same man. Circumstances brought us together and it was now in my power to make positive things happen. I had been given an opportunity which came from our ravagings. It was somewhat like we were getting back at "D" for what he had done to us. After I ran my proposal by Li'l M, the tears started flowing.

"I never thought I would amount to much, but because of you Miss Pierre and this opportunity, I am going to do my best to do something grand for the less fortunate," she said. "What you have started with your generosity will be multiplied. I will work so hard and when I get totally on my feet, I will in turn give back and put forward. I will do you proud."

I told Li'l M it will take some time to find the right location and used piano and then we would need to get the word out about our business. Until that time, and until she was fully healed, she would need to tend to the cooking and cleaning and laundering around our little home. The look of awe-struck gratitude beamed from her face. She graciously said, "That would all be wonderful." She promised me that she would work very hard and never let me down. I also said there was one other stipulation. She said, "Sure Miss Pierre whatever it is you want..." I cut her off before she could finish her sentence.

"You will have to open a bank account and put at least $4,000 into it," I said. "You need to start to make a little nest egg for yourself and be able to take care of yourself with this money."

She said of course she would do that if that is what I wanted her to do. I said one last thing needs to be figured out—we need a name for our business. I told her that we should both think about that for a couple days and see what we came up with.

When I went to TCA to ask him if I could have this

little business, he said he would have to think things over and he would get back to me. I was a bit nervous that maybe he wasn't going to let this all happen. My worries faded when I received a beautiful green business style suit from a local storekeeper. In the box there was a card that simply read, "To my angel, who is now going to be a very successful business woman."

Six months went by and we found a small storefront area right in the heart of the Quarter that was for rent. We moved the used piano we found into the area. Some furniture and lovely touches made our business feel more like a home. We had Handy Holly make us curtains and table cloths and reupholster some of the furniture to match our beautiful Mardi Gras theme. It was the essence of New Orleans all done in the colors of green, gold and purple. Our place was regal yet comfortable and inviting. We were hoping to be open for business within the next two months. The only thing we were lacking was the name of our business. We needed that so that we could have all of the proper legal documents drawn up and so that we could advertise our services.

I was so very busy at this time in my life, still performing at the clubs and houses while helping out when I had time to get the business ready for our grand opening. But I needed to stay busy as I found that I was thinking more and more about my son. I wondered where he was and prayed to God that he was okay. I kept telling myself that someday I would find him. I just didn't know how or when, but I had faith in God that it would happen for me. Li'l M was doing very well both physically and emotionally. She was so excited about getting our business off the ground and was spending hours practicing on our new, used piano. She was able to keep up with her chores at our house as well. She was true to her word – she did not let me down in any way.

Everything was moving forward very smoothly. Erina and Holly were always at our house or at the business when they had spare time. One evening, Li'l M, Irene, Erina and Holly all got together at our house for some cheer. We were celebrating mine and Li'l M's upcoming grand opening when Erina told us about a man who was found dead at one of the houses. It was a gruesome scene. One of the clients who was with a young girl was killed by a beautiful be-jeweled chandelier that had fallen on top of him. The main stem of the crystal chandelier went right through his neck and pinned him onto the bed. It broke his neck and he bled out which killed him. Erina had heard that when they went to remove the chandelier it looked like it was a necklace around his neck by the way the crystals from the chandelier were lying after the impact. She went on to say that she heard the man was a wealthy plantation owner from Mississippi and that people had seen him in that house and other houses over the past several years. He was tall and very well dressed with dark hair. He had a reputation for being rough with the ladies, but because of his power and wealth, the Madams of the houses still let him come in. When the police arrived to the scene after The Madam of the House called them, they said they went into his billfold. There were documents in there that identified him as being Damas DuMonde from Mississippi. I didn't flinch when I heard the name but found a strange sense of freedom and empowerment. Erina even said that some speculated it was the same man who had done the terrible beating to Li'l M. Many of the girls were relieved to know that this man had died. Somehow the chandelier came undone from the ceiling. Some even joked that it came loose from how hard the bed was banging the wall earlier in the night from the activity that was going on in the room. When they questioned the young girl who had been with him, she said that she left the room to go and get soap and clean water as he had wanted her to clean him up. She said when she heard the loud crash, she came running back into the room along with a few of the other girls and the Madam of the House. The police said it was an accident. For a brief moment, I thought about wrapping up the night's festivities as Li'l M might need some time alone to herself to think about what she had just heard and to let it all run through her. I was surprised by how well she handled this information. She asked me if she could talk to me for a minute in private. We went out to our little courtyard.

"Miss Pierre, I know in my heart and soul that the man that Erina was talking about is the man who raped and beat me," she said. "I have to say I feel a sense of relief in knowing that he can never find me or hurt me again. I know it is wrong to wish ill will on people, but I am willing to take God's wrath for my contentment at hearing he has been punished for his misdeed."

I have to say I felt exactly the same way as her, but I never said a word. I asked her if we should end the night and she said "Hell no, it is a time for celebration. I am free of the demons that have been haunting me since that night. I feel as though I am now free." I stood there for a minute and I thought I too was feeling the same exact feeling. I put my hands on her shoulders and said "Well then—"Laissez les bons temps rouler!"

We all stayed up quite late that night and after Erina and Holly left, Li'l M and I sat down and I said, "How do you feel about our business name being named Liberté?"

She said, "That word means freedom?" I told her that it did and she said, "I can't think of a better name Miss Pierre— Liberté!"

I never asked Frankie if he had something to do with the demise of "D" but I had a feeling he did. I tried not to think of all of the implications that would have and if I was then somewhat responsible for what happened. But I was able to work it out in my mind, heart and soul that this was not on my conscience. I remembered thinking to myself it is funny how we all tell ourselves little lies to get by. I started to replay things in my mind and I wondered if "D" had possibly seen me performing at one of the places I was working at over the past several years. He obviously never approached me and I thank God for that. That could have taken my life on a totally different course and I may have then taken matters in to my own hands. But at that time, I convinced myself that my hands were clean.

LIBERTÉ

A couple of years passed by. Liberté was doing very well. We had obtained a good business reputation amongst the people of money who lived in the Quarter. Most of the people who came to us for piano and singing lessons were children of the more wealthy pillars of our community. Li'l M was working five days a week with at least two to three lessons a day. One afternoon both Li'l M and I had just finished up giving lessons for the day. There was a knock at the front door and Li'l M went to answer it. When she came back into our parlor, she was in the company of a beautifully dressed, statuesque woman. I remember thinking she was wearing the most beautiful outfit I had ever seen. The skirt she was wearing was made of materials I couldn't even identify. I said to her, "Hello, can we help you?"

She replied in a very eloquent voice, "Why yes, I believe you can. My name is Flordie and I am the Head Mistress at a local educational institution only two blocks from your business. I have been hearing wonderful things about the two of you and what a wonderful job you are doing teaching several of our students singing and piano lessons. I am not here to tell you both how wonderful you are but to ask you a favor."

I looked at Li'l M and thought she may be thinking the same thing I was—we were intrigued by this woman and wanted to hear what it was she wanted.

"Miss Flordie, I can't imagine what we can possibly do for you but please go on," I said.

She continued on to say that there were some other children in this neighborhood she knew of who couldn't afford to pay our fees for our lessons. However, she felt that they too deserved a chance at trying to better their lives by having our lessons. She asked if there would be any way we could consider letting these children come in on off hours or whenever we could fit them in? She said she had some money she could use to pay for these lessons, but since there were four children she had in mind for this special service, it may be too much for her to afford paying the standard rate. She offered that in exchange for our services, she would give us an established amount of money each month and she could also provide us with little treats that could be given as a lagniappe to our regular customers. She explained that she had a little side business making sweets for a local bakery in the neighborhood. The three of us just stood there staring at each other not knowing what to say.

I quickly gathered my thoughts and said, "Please give us a moment to go and discuss your proposal in the back room. Please have a seat and we will be back in a few minutes."

Li'l M and I both broke out in stifled laughs at this entire scene. We were floored by Flordie! But we both looked at each other and nodded. We quickly talked about her proposal and we realized how blessed we were to even have our little business and that if we could give back in someway, it would be the right thing to do. We also discussed how absolutely beautiful her outfit was and what a presence she had. We were spellbound by Miss Flordie and felt that we couldn't say no.

We went back out into the parlor and I said to her, "Miss Flordie, we are accepting your proposal. We will offer our lessons to the students you are asking us to take on. We will accept your offer of the gratuitous sweets to be available to all of our customers including your four special students. There is one stipulation that you must agree to or the deal is off."

Miss Flordie looked a bit nervous. "What is the stipulation ladies?"

"We will not take any of your money," I replied. "It is obvious to us that you must care a great deal for these children or you wouldn't have come here. If you can be so generous and giving, we can do the same."

Miss Flordie breathed a sigh of relief and thanked us both.

"I think this is going to be a good fit for all of us," Miss Flordie said. "You have done my heart good and I won't forget this."

She surprised us when she embraced both of us at the same time. She asked us to decide on a schedule for when we would like her to drop off the sweets. She also asked if she could bring the four children to meet us the following week. I told her that would be a good idea and we set up the following Monday right after school classes let out. We walked her to the door and I said, "Do you mind if I inquire where you purchased the beautiful skirt you have on?" She told us that she found it down on Magazine Street. She said it was something she just had to have. Miss Flordie left and Li'l M and I talked about our going to Magazine Street to the shop where Miss Flordie purchased her skirt. It was autumn and we were planning on having a party for all of our customers for the Christmas Holiday. We knew that we most likely would not be able to afford purchasing that skirt but we also thought perhaps there would be something in the shop that we just had to have but could also afford.

The following Monday came quickly, and Miss Flordie and four youngsters were at Liberté right on time with three boxes. When we were all in the parlor, Miss Flordie introduced each of the youngsters to us. Their names were Chester—a very Irish looking lad with ginger hair; Johnny—a tall thin teenager; a young dark-haired girl named Tawyaina who also went by the nickname Tee; and a shy, pretty girl named Faith. Flordie explained that Chester and Faith were siblings.

They all said in unison, "Miss Pierre and Miss Li'l M, we are very thankful for your willingness to give us piano and singing lessons."

Li'l M and I were so impressed with these children. They were all clean and dressed in what looked to be their Sunday best. They were so polite and innocent. Li'l M and I quickly fell in love with them. Johnny was the oldest out of the group by quite a few years. He seemed to be their protector and their leader. The other children seemed to look up to him for approval and guidance. Flordie said that she didn't want to keep us too long and we set up the date for their first lessons, which would be later in the week. She also insisted that we just call her Flordie as that is what she said everyone calls her. Flordie picked up the boxes she had brought and handed them to Li'l M and myself. She explained that the top box was filled with sweet treats. She said the other two boxes had treats in them but of a different kind. She gathered up her young belongings and they were on their way. Right after they left, Li'l M and I excitedly opened the two other boxes. We couldn't believe our eyes! Inside each box was our own beautiful skirt, an exact replica of the one Flordie had been wearing when we first met. She had gauged our sizes perfectly. We both hugged each other and I said to Li'l M, "A dream has come true. We both have a beautiful new skirt to wear to our holiday party—a skirt we could never have afforded on our own."

I remembered back to when I first came to New Orleans and saw all the beautifully dressed women and how I wanted to someday be like them—so poised, polished and assured. By my having this skirt, I felt I too was becoming the woman I could be. It is funny how a simple article of clothing can hold that much power in its delicate threads. Perhaps the clothes don't make the person. But they can make the person wearing them, aspire to be the best they can be. Flordie's generosity did that for me.

A few months went by and we were totally enjoying our time with the YP's. That is the affectionate name we gave to our four young protégé's. It was so endearing to watch them all interact with each other. We didn't know any of the financial situations these children came from and that didn't matter to us. What mattered is that they were so appreciative of the singing and piano lessons given by myself and Li'l M. To show their appreciation, they would bring us beautiful hand assembled bouquets of different colored roses, but mostly pink ones, that we assumed they must have picked from the beautiful gardens around the city. We couldn't believe that they were able to find these magnificent flowers each time they came for a lesson. We particularly loved the fragrances they emitted throughout Liberté. We knew it was their way of showing their gratitude to us, but what they didn't realize was that we were so thankful for them. They made our day. Their hunger for the knowledge of music was so captivating. I have to say that after only three months, these youngsters were becoming quite good. Johnny was the most talented of the bunch and I took such a shine to him. He was tall for his age and even though he was not yet a man, he seemed to have such a good head on his shoulders. I remember thinking he would be right around the same age as my son.

What was even more heartfelt was the shine that Johnny seemed to be taking to young Tee. Those two became inseparable. We did have a small grand opening ceremony when we first opened Liberté, but now that we were more well established, we were moving forward with our plans for our holiday party. We invited all of our friends and customers. When Flordie found out we were having this event, she graciously offered to provide all of the sweets for the event. She told us that she recently hired Faith to work with her on her little side business. She said that Faith seemed to have a talent for baking and cooking and just loved to spend time in Flordie's kitchen putting together delectable, confectionary delights. Flordie also said she would like to decorate it beautifully for the holiday party, if we would allow her to do so. We were so excited that she offered to do this for us and couldn't think of a reason not to accept her offer. We told her that we would very much appreciate that and we even asked her if she would wear her beautiful skirt, the same one she purchased for us. We would all be dressed in the same beautiful skirt with different colored tops for the evening. We were all very much looking forward to the night's festivities. We had also planned to have the YP's performing many of the evening's Christmas carols. Our holiday party was the talk of our town. When we heard from so many people that they would be attending, we rented out the back of the building, which was just a storage area for the business next door. They let us move their supplies off to a side room and we also used that space.

Flordie did an outstanding job of decorating all of the rooms. People said they felt like it was walking into a winter wonderland done New Orleans style! We couldn't believe how many people actually showed up that evening. The sweets provided by Flordie and Faith were devoured by our guests, and much to our surprise, so many of the people who attended also brought a dish to share. There was so much food, and of course, drinks. TCA took care of that for us. He didn't actually attend the festivities but he had let me know that he wanted to contribute in some-way – and that was his way. We all had a wonderful time. It was magical. The night went by so fast. After our last guests left and it was just myself, Li'l M, the CC's and Miss Margaret, we started the daunting task of cleaning every-thing up. We were so appreciative of all that Flordie had done for us, we told her to please just leave everything. We would get all of her beautiful Christmas dishes that she had brought all cleaned up for her and she could pick them up in a day or two.

She just looked at us and laughed and said, "My ladies, the Christmas dishes are my gift to you. Keep them well as they are very special to me. But the friendship we have developed is even more special to me. I would like for you to have them. Merry Christmas."

Later that night when I laid my head down on my pil-low, I started to cry. I couldn't stop thinking about what the Christmas dishes that Flordie gave to us meant to me. They brought back those beautiful memories of myself with my mother and the special dishes we would use for our holiday parties. It was all so bittersweet. I also remem-bered the poem I had written for her. I actually still had a copy of that poem in my bedroom. I pulled it out and read it to myself. I felt that the gift of the dishes was a sign.

I would need to do something with my poem rather than just have it sit in a box. I knew I would someday. I also thought of my good fortune with Liberté. I believe TCA must have played some role in our success with Liberté, but I was just so pleased that there was money coming in and I actually had become a businesswoman. I was even more pleased to see Li'l M become a different person. She couldn't have been more appreciative to me and to God.

LACE AROUND THE MOON

It was getting a bit late in the day and Mr. Baynes asked me if I wanted to stop for the day or take a break. I told him that I really felt I had it in me to go on a bit further as I really wanted to talk about the next phase of my life as I could remember it all so clearly. So, we continued on …

One evening when I was alone in my courtyard, I looked up at the beautiful full moon and I remembered the parting words that Sister Veronica said to me when she sent me off to go and live at the cottage. Her words kept repeating themselves over and over in my mind – "Whenever you look up and see the lace around the moon, know that our hearts will be together soon." When I looked at the moon through the leaves on the trees, I actually remember saying out loud, 'I see it, I see the lace around the moon.'" I then knew what Sister Veronica was talking about. The lyrics came easily and smoothly that night and I brought it to our band to see if they could write the music for it. We all worked on the song for around a month.

After we had if finalized to our satisfaction, we added it into our performances. I remember the first night TCA had heard us perform it. It was the last song of our first set. As always, he would just sit there staring at me but this time I saw him smile! He had never done that before. I felt like it was an actual gift that had just been given to me. I felt very proud of the band and my accomplishment with getting *Lace Around the Moon* to the beautiful song that we felt it was. Three days later, there was a messenger at my door with a small box. I recognized the young man as someone who I had seen with Frankie before and I knew that he worked for TCA. The box was far too small to have a dress in it and it wasn't the anniversary of mine and TCA's meeting so I couldn't imagine what was in there. I opened it up and it was a piece of paper with the name of Vincent Ladue, Esquire and his address. There was also a message, "You are to go and meet with this man. He is going to make *Lace Around the Moon* legally yours. Your song spoke to my heart. TCA."

Another few years went by and life was good. I was thankful for everything I had. But I just felt empty and lonely. I was never actually alone as my little house was quite full with Li'l M, Irene and the other ladies were always coming over for our little get-togethers. I knew what I was missing in my life and that was love. I had love for my mother and I did grow to love the CC's, but I had never known the type of love that becomes all consuming and all encompassing. I remember thinking that I should have been more careful in my prayers to God where I asked him to please send me someone to love and someone who would love me.

In my search for solace and to give thanks, Li'l M and I would go to the St. Louis Cathedral and then over to Jackson Square at least once or twice a week to go to Mass or sometimes just to light a candle and thank God for our good fortune. Also, we enjoyed listening to the new young Irish priest. Father Tommy Mulroney began saying the Masses on Sundays. He had such a powerful presence even in the large cathedral. I have to admit that I started to go to church even more often. There was something drawing me there. Sometimes during Mass, I would let my voice soar during one of the hymns. Many people would comment to me after Mass what a beautiful voice I had and that I should be a singer. I would politely thank them for their kind words. I never let on that I already was a singer as I didn't want to have to tell them where I was singing. But I did notice quite a few of the gentlemen who were at church were the same ones who would sometimes frequent the places where I was singing. We were all discrete about our associations. Who was I to judge?

I started to notice that Father Mulroney was noticing me. Sometimes he would come out of the church after

Mass and give us blessings on the church steps. He would shake my hand and comment on my beautiful voice. This went on for around six months. We never actually spoke outside of the parameters of St. Louis Cathedral. That was until one beautiful Sunday afternoon. Li'l M had an afternoon piano lesson and had to hurry to Liberté right after Mass. I walked over to Jackson Square and sat on the park bench. I enjoyed watching all of the people just going to and fro. There were high society people, all dressed in their Sunday best, and then there were the poor and street beggars. I had a little bag of treats that I would leave behind for the feral cats that lived in Jackson Square, but did not come out until night time. That Sunday, there was an older man who was walking around asking for handouts of coins. I called him over and said I couldn't give him a coin but that he could have my bag of bread scraps if he wanted them. He yanked it out of my hands so quickly that I was actually startled and he ran away. That is when I heard a familiar voice say, "Are you okay?" I turned to see Father Mulroney behind me. I was more startled to see him outside of the church than I was at having my bag ripped out of my hands. I composed myself and said, "Yes, thank you Father. I am fine."

My heart was racing and I felt I was stammering. Father Mulroney asked if he could sit down on the park bench? I said, "Of course." We both just sat there for a couple of minutes in silence. He finally said, "I love to hear your singing during Mass. Can I ask what your name is?" I replied, "Pierre."

He extended his hand out for a formal handshake. I remember thinking he must have felt my hand shaking during our first introduction and I was embarrassed. He said, "It is a pleasure to formally meet you Miss Pierre. I am Father Tommy Mulroney." He held onto my hand a little too long. I didn't mind it—I just felt there was a current going between our two hands. And the current was passing right straight through to my heart.

For the next several weeks it became my ritual. I would go to Sunday Mass and then across the way to the Jackson Square. Most of those times, Father Tommy asked me if he could join me. We would just make small talk. At first, I was so nervous to even speak to him, but then after a few weeks, it was the only thing I wanted to do. He was so knowledgeable about so many things including music and art. He was so interesting and so engaging. I couldn't help but start to want him to engage me—in something. I had such conflicting emotions about this entirely innocent friendship of sorts. I had no idea if he had any feelings for me as he was never anything more than polite. He would tell me during our talks how he found his calling to God's work as a priest. He never wanted to be anything other than God's servant going back to his very young years.

"When you know that you are destined to be a voice for the Lord, you know," he said. "I felt as though God had single handedly picked me out as one of his own."

I remembered looking at him thinking how wonderful it must be for him to have known that this was to be his life and that he was so happy to do it. I also remember thinking, how sad for me as I would have liked the opportunity to have gotten to know him on a different level. I never had those feelings before in my life. With everything I went through with "D," I never thought I would be unfrozen. Sadly, for me, Father Tommy unfroze my heart.

I found a strange sense of tranquility in spending more and more time with Li'l M and our YP's. It was both heart warming and heart hurting to be with them as often as I could. The more time I spent with them, the more I would think about my own son. I decided to go over to the Ursuline Convent, which had moved to a different part of New Orleans to visit with Sister Veronica. I had heard through Miss Margaret that her sister had been failing lately in both physical and mental health. When I arrived, sister Jolynn answered the door and hugged me when she saw it was me. She then escorted me into the main area of the convent. I told her I was so glad to see that she was doing so well. She looked healthy and happy. I wasn't expecting to even see her there as I also had heard that she was very sick. She said that she was taking care of herself and that she felt that it wasn't God's will for her to leave this world yet. She said, "God still has work down here for me to do before he will let me come home."

She did warn me that Sister Veronica was not doing well. She went and got Sister Veronica and wheeled her into the room. I was shocked by her appearance. She had lost so much weight and looked so gaunt. She reminded me so much of my sweet mother. The saddest part was that she seemed to be unaware of who I was. I said, "Sister Veronica, it's me—Pierre. Don't you remember me?" She looked confused and I felt so bad for her. I quickly thought of a way to communicate with her—I sang one of the songs that I would sing during Mass and in our living room area of the convent many years ago when I was staying there. When she heard my voice, she laid her head back in the chair and started to cry.

"I know that voice—it is a voice of an angel," she said. I said, "You are right—it is me, Pierre."

She stretched out her arms and I hugged her and laid my head on her shoulder as I had done many years before. We both cried and didn't let go of each other for quite some time. When I finally broke free from her, I said, "Sister, can I ask you some questions about the adoption of my son?" She said, "Your son was never adopted. He was given to Miss Jennifer, Mr. DuMonde's wife." I was so confused by what she was saying. It didn't make any sense. I didn't know if Sister was just confused or what she was saying was actually true. This would mean that "D" had my child that entire time—he was never adopted? How could "D" have a wife named Jennifer when he was married to my mother? How could this all be? What was even more upsetting to me was that I didn't know where to turn to find out the truth. It certainly would never come from Sister Veronica as she was not in her right mind. This was the biggest blow I ever felt since having my child taken from me. It was so unfair. My life was a series of unfortunate circumstances that led me into different paths on a road that wound up going in circles. I was beside myself with grief but didn't want to upset Sister Veronica. I stayed a bit longer and chatted with her on things that were not making any sense, but she still seemed so happy to have me there with her. I told her I had to get to work and that I would come back and visit with her again in a few weeks. I just felt the need to be out of the Ursuline Convent, away from thoughts of my prior life. I found myself going to my place of peace—I was at the Jackson Square before the sun went down.

I was sitting there on my bench, clenching my teeth with total hostility and frustration. I wanted to cry as that would have given me some release, but the tears just wouldn't come. I was just staring at the people going by when I felt him sit down next to me. He could tell something was wrong but he didn't want to pry. We both sat there in total silence and he surprised me when he took my hand. We just sat there holding hands for around ten minutes without saying a word. It was very risky for him to do such a thing as any of the church parishioners could have seen us, but he didn't seem to care. He knew I needed this connection. Such began our affair of the heart—only the heart.

We went on with our hand holding love affair for around three months. I knew I wanted more, but if that was all he could give to me, I was happy just to have that. I was in love with him and I felt he loved me back. He just seemed to have such deliberations with himself and with God and with me. One afternoon at Jackson Square, he hesitantly told me he was being reassigned to a church back in Ireland where he was originally from. He said he couldn't refuse this transfer as that was all decided by the higher-ranking members of the Catholic Church. He also told me that he was glad to be going back to County Cork, where he could spend some time with his father who was suffering from a disease that affected his lungs. He didn't know if his father had much time left and he wanted to go back and be there for his mother. I remember I put my head down and took his hand that was in mine and made him feel the tears that were welling out of my eyes.

"Other than my heart, my tears on your hand are the only part of myself that you will be taking with you when you go," I said to him.   "I am at peace with the fact that

I don't have any regrets on my soul that we ever did anything that would jeopardize your strong relationship with God. I did not make you fall in his eyes. I did want you for myself, but God's will is greater than mine. I never knew if your feelings for me are as great as mine are for you, but I need to know."

His final words to me were, "Pierre, I could never let you in because if I did, my heart would never let you go."

I sat on the park bench and watched him slowly pace himself back to St. Louis Cathedral. His steps were not purposeful but rather hesitant. I often wondered if he thought about turning around and taking me in his arms? But that did not happen. I like to think that maybe if he made a proposal such as I did many years ago in Jackson Square that perhaps his life would have also been pivotal. If only he would have turned in my direction and stayed, our two lives would have been so much different. I sat there only for a bit longer as I had to get ready to go to work. I knew Frankie would be coming for me soon. Before getting off the bench, I remember that I looked up at the moon. I quietly sang, "Whenever you look up and see the lace around the moon, know that our hearts will be together soon, with this we will never be apart." That is all I had left of my Father Tommy, just my memories of him under the moonlit sky. As I was quickly trying to get back home, I had the strangest sense of someone following me. I started to get a bit nervous and even broke into a run. There were people around but everyone was minding their own business and I wasn't quite sure what to do. It was only a feeling. I turned the corner quickly as to throw this strange presence off of my heels when I actually ran right smack into Frankie! I almost fell down but he steadied me on my feet. He said, "Miss Pierre, what are you doing over in this area all by yourself? Don't you know it is dangerous for a woman to be going down these side streets?"

I was startled to see Frankie there but also glad to see him. I tried to tell him that I thought I was being followed. He seemed concerned and said, "Don't you worry, I am here now and will keep you safe. We better go back to your home so you can get ready for me to take you to work. I will stay outside and wait for you to get ready so you don't feel scared."

I told him I so very much appreciated his being there for me. He always was. On the way home, I did ask him what he was doing in this neighborhood. He told me he lived a few streets away from where I ran into him. I remembered thinking how I was so fortunate that Frankie was there again for me in my hour of need. But for a brief moment, I did question how could it be that he was there at precisely that time? Maybe it wasn't a coincidence?

PIVOTAL CIRCUMSTANCES

My heart was broken twice that month. First my Father Tommy leaving and going back to Ireland and then by my sweet Frankie. I was getting ready for work one day and there was a knock at my door. It was a man who I knew that worked for TCA as his driver. His name was Ronnie. He looked very upset when he said, "Miss Pierre, can you please come out to the carriage, Mr. Anderson wants to speak with you." I knew something must be terribly wrong as TCA never once came to my home. I agreed to his request and Ronnie held my hand as he guided me into the seat across from TCA. I had never seen him look anything other than calm, cool and collected. That was not the case on that very sad St. Patrick's Day.

"Pierre, I wanted to be the one to tell you that Frankie was killed this morning in a roofing accident," TCA said. "He was repairing the roof on top of a building that had recently been involved in a fire. His brother Christian, a fireman in the Quarter, who was also a roofer, asked him if he could help him out for some extra money. He needed assistance with repairing the roof as it was going to be a very large job. When they were up there, they didn't realize the extent of the fire damage or they would not have risked going up on that high roof. They worked all morning up until noon, all that time pulling off burnt shingles and didn't realize until it was too late just how much damage had been done. In the area where Frankie was working, all of the anchoring beams had been damaged by the fire. Frankie fell through the three-foot hole that had evolved."

TCA started to cry. I don't know if I was more upset in seeing him cry or if I was just beside myself with grief in having just heard what he told me. I don't remember if he reached for me, or if I reached for him, but we embraced and held each other tight and just sobbed for what seemed like was an eternity, but was just for a couple of minutes. We both collected our emotions and I just sat there with my head down. So many thoughts of Frankie were going through my mind. I remember thinking, I had lost my best friend. TCA was back to his normal staunch self and said that there was going to be an Irish wake for Frankie the following weekend. He said that he was going to do it up right for Frankie and his family. He also asked me if I would get with the band and be prepared to sing *Danny Boy* toward the end of the church service and end it with *Lace Around the Moon*. I said it would be an honor and privilege to do that.

I remember thinking that whenever I looked up and saw the lace around the moon from that day forward, I would see Frankie's face silhouetted in the moon. He would forever be in my heart and in my soul. I sang my heart out for Frankie that sad day. It was such a beautiful party in Frankie's honor. I couldn't believe when I got to the hall where his wake was going to take place just how warm and welcoming it felt. It truly was a party. I commented to his family how beautiful it looked and what a wonderful spread of food had been prepared for Frankie's family and friends. I was even more in awe of the amount of beautiful fresh flowers that were placed around the entire room. I couldn't imagine where all of these roses could have come from. And that beautiful sweet smell of them is something that will always linger in my mind. I went over to TCA who was sitting at one of the tables and thanked him for doing all of this for Frankie. He looked at me inquisitively and said, "Pierre, this entire event has been catered and taken care of by your friend Flordie." I tried to pass it off as I knew that, but I honestly didn't. I couldn't believe she did all of this for Frankie's family, but now I realized she actually did it for me. All of his brothers and sisters were there and thanked me so much for giving him such a special tribute. I felt like I knew all of them because Frankie was always speaking of them in our many conversations. I spent a great deal of time that day talking with his sister Kim. She seemed to be the matriarch of the Quigley family. I also learned from them that he was always telling them about me and what a wonderful singer I was and what a wonderful friend I had become to him. At the end of the party that night, I asked everyone to raise their glasses and please join me in a toast to Frankie. I recited two old Irish blessings I had heard through the years, "May you be in heaven an hour before the devil knows your dead." The other one was, "Always remember death leaves a heartache that no one can heal. Love leaves a memory that no one can steal." Everyone raise your glass and let's toast to Frankie—your brother, your business partner, your son, your neighbor, your friend and my very dear friend."

I continued on with my life. It was full, but I was still heart empty. I missed Father Tommy but I missed my protector, Frankie, even more in some ways. I was still working at the different clubs and brothels but not as often. Actually, I was quite surprised how I was becoming even more popular especially since TCA made it possible that *Lace Around the Moon* became my song. I learned that he paid the band members a very generous amount of money so that they would not have any rights to the song. He wanted it to be mine and mine alone. It opened many doors for me. I was invited to sing at the prime entertainment supper clubs and restaurants throughout the Quarter. I gladly accepted all of those offers, but I didn't want to stop singing at the less proper places where I started off at. I never forgot where I came from and I never would. It was those experiences that shaped me into the person I became. I was first a girl from wealth and became a young woman who had to make it on her own. Don't get me wrong, there was Sister Veronica and Miss Margaret and the CC's and TCA who helped mold me into the woman I became. But I stand firm in that it was the strength I found inside myself that made me into the woman I became with the loving, guiding hand of God. I didn't always think he was in my court, but during the times I think he abandoned me, something astounding would happen to me that would make me believe he was still there—always looking after me.

I was making good money as I was being paid more to play in the clubs because I had become somewhat of celebrity in the Quarter and Storyville. One stipulation I put on all of my appearances was that if they wanted me, my band was part of the deal. Things were going well. I still spent some time at Liberté, but the "YP's" had grown up and stopped coming in for their special lessons. We still kept in contact with them. Faith was still working with Flordie on their little side business and Flordie actually had rented out space just a couple of blocks from Liberté.

They opened up a little sweet shop and it was called, "La-gniappe Bon Appetit!" Chester was also doing well and was trying to get into the Police Department. They would all occasionally stop in and see us at Liberté. We would all get together there and Li'l M and Johnny would take turns playing on the piano while Chester, Faith, Tee and I would all sing along. Those were unforgettable times to me. They were precious. Johnny had become an exceptional piano player and he had a wonderful, enchanting singing voice. I asked our band members if they would do a favor for me and let him come and audition for the band as Jacob, our band leader was planning on leaving as he was getting up in age and wanted to spend more time at home. Keep in mind, we had a very grueling schedule for many years and it can take a toll on a person's home life. Our piano player, Jeremy, would step up and become band leader and we needed a backup vocal singer and piano player. Out of respect for me they did let him audition. I think they had a preconceived notion that he would just be another piano player and singer from the Quarter and they would appease me by letting him have the audition. I was so glad when I actually saw a couple of the band members start to put even more enthusiasm into their playing while he was performing. Johnny inspired them to be the best they could be. After he performed just three songs, we asked him to go and get a drink and come back in around an hour. After he left, I didn't have to even ask what they thought. Band leader Jeremy looked at the other members who all nodded. He then said, "He is in. I believe we will have a resurgence. He is just what we needed to breathe new life into us."

We welcomed Johnny into our band family. We also welcomed Tee as she and Johnny were now husband and wife with a little one on the way. Occasionally we would have Tee perform with our band when we were doing special appearances or when I was not able to make the performance. Both of them became one of us and for the next few years, things were good. They were very good. They were profoundly good.

Things really started to change for me a couple of years later. I had heard the talk around town that TCA had gotten in trouble with the law. Real trouble this time. I actually was surprised when one day, one of the YP's, Chester came into Liberté and asked if he could talk official business with me. It had been a couple of years since I last saw him. I almost didn't recognize him in his official police attire. He was just as sweet as he was when he was younger as he gave me an all encompassing hug and kiss on my cheek. But he now had a different presence about him. I was so proud to see him stand so tall and purposeful in his position as a law enforcement officer, but was also very speculative as to why he was there to see me in an official capacity. He asked if we could sit down. I said, "Of course, Chester. Is there something wrong?"

He looked me straight in the eyes and said, "Miss Pierre, I have nothing but adoration and respect for you. You have been wonderful to me since I first met you years ago when I first started to come here to Liberté. I always remember thinking when I was growing up that I wish I had someone like you as my mother because my actual mother was never really around for me. She was a prostitute, and Faith and I had a hard life. I believe she loved us in her own way, she just never had the means or ability to guide us. If you, Li'l M and Miss Flordie hadn't been in my life when you all were with the singing lessons and the civility and compassion you showed us, I don't think I would be here today. I wouldn't have been taught what hard work, perseverance and dedication can do for a person. You all taught me discipline but with love and nurturing. I want you to know that it was because of you, Li'l M and Miss Floridie, I am the man I have become. Please don't think I was oblivious to all the rumors I heard growing up about who our father may have been, but that is irrelevant to what I need to tell you now. I need your promise that you will never tell anyone that I gave you the information I am about to give to you."

I was very bewildered by our entire conversation, but I agreed to his request simply because I felt so sorry for him as I could see the turmoil he was having by taking the risk of speaking to me.

"Chester, I have never known you to be anything other than truthful and honest in the years we have known each other," I said. "I don't believe you would ever put me at risk in any way as I do believe that we have a bond. And if you are here to tell me something that you need for me to know, I will respect your request and not speak of it to anyone."

"I always have known that you have been working in different brothels, pleasure clubs and speakeasies," he continued. "I also know through the Police Department and just street talk that you work for TCA. You need to know that for many years, law enforcement has turned a blind eye to all of his unscrupulous activities. However, we are no longer able to cover for him or look the other way. He has recently been charged with operating a lewd establishment within ten miles of a military base and for having forty prostitutes working for him. Miss Pierre, with all you have accomplished in your life, I just don't want your good name to get dragged down with him. I am asking you to separate yourself from him, before he brings you down with him. I am more than asking you, I am letting you know that you may also be looking at facing some charges if you are found to be working in one of these establishments when he is brought down. I am risking my career by telling you this. But I feel I owe it to you as you have always looked out for me. I am now doing the same for you."

I got up from my chair and he did the same. I reciprocated his hug and said, "My dearest Chester, I will never betray your confidence in all that you have just told me. I can see how much you have deliberated about coming to me with this information. I am so proud of you and my heart is swelling with pride to have known you when you were young and now as the man you evolved into. I know what you have told me is for my own good and I will have to think over everything you said. I don't want to expound on my relationship with TCA with you as that would put us both in a questionable predicament. We will go on as if this conversation never happened. Please leave here knowing you have done everything you could to look out for me without anyone ever knowing you did."

I remember that night after Chester had come to see me that I didn't sleep until the morning. I just kept thinking over and over about the relationship I had with TCA and I couldn't possibly think of a way of my telling him that I wanted to leave him. I also didn't understand what Chester meant by him saying that he wasn't oblivious to who his and Faith's father may have been. So many wild thoughts were running through my mind; so many unanswered questions. I was finally able to sleep after I had drowned my many sorrows in my whiskey and no longer could keep my head up and my mind finally shut down along with my body. The next morning when I woke up things were clearer. I knew what Chester told me made sense. I couldn't risk ruining my reputation and all I had built for myself with my continued association with TCA. However, I had no idea how I could ever go to TCA and tell him that I couldn't work for him anymore. If it had not been for him and all that he did for me, I wouldn't have most of the things I had in my life. It was because of him that I had my career, my song and Liberté. But most importantly, I had my essence of being. He put me on a pedestal and I so wanted to stay there. I wanted to be his everything without ever actually being his anything. How many women can say that they had a man in their life for many, many years who never wanted them in a womanly way, but still wanted and needed them there just as much as if they had been their woman in every aspect of their life? Our relationship was complicated because it endured the test of time without ever testing the waters of what might have been. It took some time before I was able to get the courage up to get word to him that I needed to speak to him—that it was very important. I sent word out through the different clubs I was still performing at that I could meet him wherever he wanted me to as I knew he was keeping a very low profile and didn't want to be seen in any type of scandalous establishment. I had never done that before and I wasn't surprised when I didn't hear back that he would agree to meet me.

Other things were weighing heavily on my mind that I needed answers to. I thought that the only person who could possibly shed some light on some of the nagging questions I had after Chester came to visit me would be Flordie. After all, she was the one who brought the YP's into our lives. I went over to her house to see if we could talk. However, her husband told me that she was out of town visiting her sister and wouldn't be back for a few weeks.

By that time, TCA's trial had started and it made all of the newspapers. It did cast an unfavorable light around him and all of his associates. He had denied all of the charges that were brought against him and the trial did end in a mistrial. But by then, the damage had already been done. I had heard he would no longer associate himself with prostitution in any manner.

I started to think that maybe I was spared the heart wrenching task of ending our relationship as a few months went by without any communication from him or any of his associates. I did start to get nervous that perhaps my days were numbered in the singing establishments I was still performing at throughout the city. However, that was not the case. I was still asked to perform at the places I was currently working at and even at different places I couldn't believe I would ever have been invited to perform at. Another few weeks went by and I received a hand-written note slid under my door. On the piece of paper it simply read "Be at the Metairie Cemetery Friday afternoon at 4:00pm." I was a bit apprehensive about going as I only speculated it was TCA who was requesting my presence. I felt I had no choice but to go. When I arrived there, I was greeted by the Groundskeeper who told me his name was Richard.

He said, "Miss Pierre it is an honor to meet you. I have been listening to you and your band for many years and I have seen you perform many times. I have been instructed to take you over to a portion of the cemetery where someone is waiting to see you." It was a bit of a walk over to where Richard left me. He said, "I will be back for you in around 20 minutes, Miss Pierre. I will help escort you back out to the main road."

I thanked him and just stood there for a minute or so before I saw him come walking towards me. My heart actually had a flutter. I finally admitted to myself that all of these years I could have been in love with him if he had ever opened that door. He asked me to please sit down next to him on a little bench that I speculated was placed there for just this occasion.   He had a bottle of whiskey and two glasses. He poured us each a drink. He told me that the crypt we were in front of was his family's. He would eventually be buried there with all of his relatives, it would be his final resting place. He then said, "Pierre you obviously know about the trail and you have known all along about my involvement in many underground activities. I have always looked out for you and had your best interest in mind. But now for varying reasons, I won't be. I am giving you your freedom. You are totally in charge of your life and your career moving forward. You have been the woman I respect most in my life and always know you will forever be in my mind and in my heart. You are my angel."

He clinked his glass next to mine in a toast and said, "Liberté—to your freedom! I am a man of few words when it comes to you Pierre. I find it hard to leave your presence, but have never trusted myself to stay in your presence for too long as I may have not ever been able to walk away from you. The relationship I have had with you starting back when you were a very young woman up to today has been the most fulfilling and cherished one in my life. I never wanted to ruin that for myself."

He put his glass down on the bench and I went to shake his hand, but he put his arms around me and kissed me on my cheek. I didn't even have time to reciprocate the embrace as he quickly walked away with his head down. I could feel his sadness. I too felt sadness in knowing that our paths may not cross again. However, I also felt a bit of excitement in that for the first time in my life, I was my own woman—totally free. I sat there for a few minutes not sure what to do. I was reeling from so many emotions. Thankfully, Richard came back and said he was going to escort me out, but before he would do that, he had to show me something. He asked me to follow him over to the next crypt. Etched into the stone were the simple words "My Angel." The word "My" was on one line and then there was a space between the next word "Angel", which was on the line below. I said, "I don't understand Richard, what does this mean?" He explained to me that someone had purchased this crypt for me.

"Miss Pierre, you are under no obligation to be buried here when your time to go has come," he said. "However, the person who has purchased it for you would be honored if you were to lay next to him through eternity."

I couldn't believe this gesture. Was it a selfish one or selfless? I just didn't know. I asked Richard why would this "someone" purchase for me such an expensive crypt? He didn't answer my question, but he pointed to a tree that was planted off to the side of the cemetery that provided shade for the area of the cemetery where these two crypts were.

"Several years back, this Southern Live Oak was dug up from where it was previously growing in another part of the cemetery," he said. "It was replanted here for the specific reason that if anyone were to look up to the moon, they would be able to see the lace around it. I think you now understand."

SEASONS OF CHANGE

The CC's were also getting older and couldn't or didn't want to continue on with their original careers. Irene met a man named Tommy who basically swept her off her feet—or should I say boots. He married her and said he made, "an honest woman out of her." Irene told me that Tommy still insisted that she wear her boots to bed whenever they were knock-in boots. He was a good man and he made her happy.

Handy Holly went on to live with and be the companion to one of the biggest cotton growers in all of Louisiana. He loved her special talents but he was captivated by her seamstress skills even more. He never married Holly. However, he purchased a building in Baton Rouge not far from his cotton plantation for Holly. He set her up in business with a garment factory. What I admired most about Holly was that she would put women who no longer wanted to be in "the working girl" business into a respectable profession as garment workers. She was the Madam of her factory, but the only thing she was selling was clothing. She never had to lie on her back again for money.

Erina also tired of her profession. She went on to Tulane University and earned a degree from their Public Health department and dedicated her life to counseling. She used all the experience she had gained from her many years with the women on the streets and she drew from her own personal experiences. She wanted to make a difference in the lives of the women who were considered to be not worthy of care simply because of the choices they made or were forced to make in their lives. Since she had lived their trials and tribulations, she was able to put so much of herself into her studies and eventually her accreditation. She found such satisfaction in the new direction her life had evolved into. It just took her a longer journey to find it. I later found out that she banked every dollar she could from the time she was one of Miss Margaret's special girls. That is what she used to pay for her education. Perhaps that was her plan all along. She knew exactly what she was doing. She just took pause for a portion of her life and went on to change so many of the lives of the people who came to her for emotional healing. She definitely lived up to her nickname of "The Healer."

Miss Margaret was true to her word. She did sell me the Courtesan Cottage. She was getting up in age and had enough of the life she had been involved in for many years. Also, after her sister, Sister Veronica had passed away, she actually went on to become a nun. She was able to stay on in New Orleans and actually went to live and work at the Ursuline Convent. She came full circle in her life. I remember thinking that not many people could say that in their lifetime they could actually have lived two totally separate lives. Miss Margaret went through all of the necessary training and became Sister Margaret. Like I said before, there is not much difference between a whore house and a convent.

I was starting to wind down. I moved into the Courtesan Cottage and changed the name to the "Comradery Cottage." I thought it was a very fitting name as it means roommate or companion. Although it was just Li'l M and I living there, the name fit. She was my roommate, but she was also my best friend.

With TCA not having any type of hold on me, I was able to make up my own schedule. I thought I could finally devote my time to working on my poem *Christmas Dishes* that I gave to my mother many years ago. I wanted to turn it into a song. I thought it over for a long time before I asked Li'l M if we could have a talk about our future. I explained to her that I would be spending less and less time with Liberté as I had other things I wanted to accomplish. I told her I still wanted to be in a partnership with her but asked her to consider adding on a third person to our partnership. Then if things went well, I would eventually like it if they would buy me out of my third of the company. I knew she had become good friends with Tee. Tee was very sharp and very smart. She was wise beyond her years and she also had a keen street sense. She was nobody's fool. I had to admit that I may have actually been a bit jealous of her as she reminded me of a younger version of myself. She had recently been singing at different clubs in the Quarter and still performing with our band on special occasions, but she was struggling. She just didn't have name recognition or anyone to guide her. Johnny did help her out, but he was very busy with our band. Tee needed her own name recognition, in her own right. I thought that if we brought her on as a third partner and if she continued to perform with us whenever possible with our band, she could possibly get the break I knew she was so longing for. When I told all of this to Li'l M she was shocked but so happy to hear what I was saying. She told me that she had always thought that Tee could really go places, but she never wanted to bring it up to me.

"Li'l M, it is hard to be moving through life knowing that you are getting older and that you can't always hold onto what was," I said. "I am at a place in my life where I am secure enough to start letting go. I have had a good run and I am not saying I am not going to continue moving forward, I just want to step quickly rather than run."

Li'l M did point out that Tee wouldn't have the financial ability to buy into the partnership. But she also said, "I remember a young girl who literally didn't have a leg to stand on, but there was someone who came into her life and turned it around. I want to do for Tee what that person did for me—give me the space to grow into the woman I was meant to be. That person was you Pierre, you were my savior."

Li'l M said she would be willing to lend Tee the money she would need from the money I had her put away many years ago. She also said she would have to run all of this by Tee before we could finalize any plans, but she was quite confident that Tee would be so excited by this prospect. She said that even though her and Johnny's daughter Maria was still young and Johnny was so busy with the band, she felt Tee would embrace this opportunity with much enthusiasm, gratitude and she would give it her all.

Li'l M had become the woman I always imagined she could be. I was even more surprised when she said to me that she was going to change her name. She wanted to totally let go of her past. She said she would like to be called "Maggie" from now on. Maggie continued to live with me for around a year. Things were going very well in our three-way partnership with myself, Maggie and Tee. So well that they were able to buy me out of the partnership sooner than I thought. It was time. Maggie had become quite astute with her investments and finances. She was able to purchase the entire building where we had been renting the space for Liberté. She had the back of the building renovated so that it became a comfortable apartment for herself. She had never lived on her own before and felt that this was what she needed to do for herself. She was finally standing strong and tall on both feet. I was very happy for her. She too was now her own person. When she finally had her apartment all set up and decorated, she asked me to please come over and see her handy work. We had a wonderful time just talking about the past and of all the plans she was making for her future. When I was getting ready to leave, she said, "Pierre I owe you my life. I want to thank you by doing something I believe will really matter to you and speak to your heart." There was a large box in the corner that was wrapped in beautiful paper with a bow on it. She asked me to open it. In the box was the other half of the Christmas dishes that Flordie had given us many years ago. I started to cry and she held me. She said, "I know what these dishes mean to you and that is why you must have the complete set." I told her I would accept her generous gift and I let her know it was the most wonderful gift I had ever been given, especially because it came from her.

I kept busy for the next several years, and although I wouldn't say I was totally happy in life, I was content. It was around that time that I got word that TCA had passed away. It was actually Sister Margaret who told me. I felt she thought that she should be the one to tell me as it was her who actually was responsible for TCA being such a large part of my life. It was because of her association with him that I was given my first real singing job. I never really thought before how it came about that back those many years ago, he decided "to take me under his wing." In speaking with her that day, I learned that she was the one who went to TCA and asked him to consider furthering my singing career. I asked her why she took it upon herself to do that for me? Why would she be so generous to do such a thing and take such a big gamble on me?

She simply replied, "Pierre, sometimes you just know when someone has been given a gift from God. And if that person doesn't have the ways or means to do something about it, and you do, it would be a sin not to let that gift be shared with others. God knows I am guilty of many sins, but with this act of my going to him on your behalf, I felt I was righting so many of my wrongs. Look at all the lives you have changed with your voice Pierre. You became my redemption."

THE BERRY-PICKER
HOUSE MURDER TRIAL

At the last meeting Gregory Baynes and I were going to be having, it made sense that we would discuss the Berry-Picker House Murder and Trial. As we sat on the park bench at Jackson Square, he said, "Miss Pierre, I have gathered some information on how it came to be that you were involved in this sensational murder trial back in Central New York. But I need to hear it all from you."

This time I didn't close my eyes, I needed them wide open so that I could feel like I was looking back to just a few months ago. I started to explain it all to him...

When Storyville was coming to its end, I was still performing at saloons and pleasure clubs both in the Quarter and in Storyville. I was just finishing up our first set one evening with *Lace Around the Moon*, when a very young man approached me. He had been paying enough attention to know that I would welcome a whiskey—neat. He asked me if he could talk to me about my music. He also wanted to know more about *Lace Around the Moon*. He said the words spoke right to his heart. He went on to tell me that his name was Phillip Wilcox and that he was from a small town in the Finger Lakes region of Central New York called Naples. It wasn't the proper time for us to get into a long discussion as I had to get ready for my next set. He then asked me if he could pay me for my time in discussing what Jazz music was all about and how I was living it. I was quite taken aback by him and his proposal. But with the substantial amount of money he was offering, I found I couldn't resist. I told him that my bandmate Jeremy would also need to come along with us and he didn't have any problem with that.

We met him a day or two later in front of Mahogany Hall. We took Phillip all over Storyville and into different pleasure clubs where the real Jazz was being played and lived. We had a wonderful time. He was so appreciative and genuinely interested in what I had to say. We stayed out quite late and by the end of the evening we were all exhausted. Before we parted ways, I extended my hand for a farewell handshake. I was quite surprised when he boldly kissed my hand. No one had ever done that since TCA many years ago. He then placed my hand on his heart and much to my surprise, he repeated the words to my song, "Whenever you look up and see the lace around the moon, know that our hearts will be together soon." I was so over come with emotions by this gesture that I took off my precious strands of glass beads that I always wore, the gift from TCA and gave them to him as parting gift.

Phillip told me that after he returned home, he would be heading off to law school. We didn't make arrangements to write to each other when we parted ways, but not long thereafter, his letters started to come to me. We developed a friendship through letter writing over the next 16 years. I sometimes thought of him as a son and confidant. We were living in two different worlds, hundreds of miles apart, but we were connected through *Lace Around the Moon*, and what the song meant.

One day, I received a telegram from Phillip's twin sister Anna. In the message, she asked if I could please come to Naples, NY and be there for support for Phillip and for her. She didn't go into all the specifics, but she said they both desperately needed me. Anna said she would pay for my transportation there. Since I was no longer singing in the Clubs except for special appearances, I did have the time. I could do this. I wasn't sure it was something I wanted to do at this point in my life, but her message spoke to my heart. I sent a telegram back and said I would be there within a week.

When I arrived there, Anna picked me up at the train terminal and explained the terrible situation to me. She started to cry and I put my arm around her and said,

"Child just take a breath. Let's pull over to the side of the road as you need to collect yourself and I need to know what happened."

She explained that Phillip had fallen in love with a young girl named Carmelita. She was one of the berry-pickers who was staying at the Berry-Picker House. Phillip found out she was pregnant and he assumed it was his child. However, Carmelita told him that it was not his. She said it was her young lover Ritchie's child. Phillip lost his mind and in a fit of rage, he took a shovel and killed her with it. They arrested Phillip for Carmelita's murder and he was put in jail awaiting his trial. I spent the next few months leading up to the trail at the main house on the Wilcox property. I would go and spend time with Phillip sitting outside of his cell and I became his confessor. And Phillip became mine. I told him things that I never told anyone. I told him how I felt responsible for "D's" death and about my entire life in New Orleans. But the one thing I never could tell him was that I had a son. I learned things about Phillip I wished I had not, but we were connected. I felt that I was in the right place being there with him during this turbulent time. I remember thinking that I had so much heartache over the entire situation. I was so sad for the family of Carmelita and for Ritchie, who lost his love. But I knew I had to be strong for Phillip and for Anna.

The trial started and was over quite quickly. No one expected things to turn out the way they did. Ritchie learned that the child he thought was his, actually turned out to be Phillip's. I was in total shock when Ritchie also lost his mind and killed Phillip by stabbing him in his back with his trimming shears. It was like I was watching a silent movie unfold right before my eyes.

The hardest part of this entire ordeal for me was when Anna and I had Phillip's burial down by the tree, the same tree on the Wilcox property where Phillip had taken Carmelita's lifeless body and was holding her when the police arrived. I learned that Phillip had given the beads that TCA had given to me to his precious Carmelita. She was holding them when Phillip killed her and they fell and broke on the floor of the Berry-Picker House. It turns out that Anna had picked those beads up after the murder. I was astounded when she took my beads out of her pocket-book and placed them on Phillip's casket at the end of the very brief burial ceremony. It was a feeling of closure for me. I was letting go of my past and all that had taken place over the past few months. They needed to be with Phillip - wherever his spirit and soul was. I tried not to dwell on all of that. I knew I had to be getting back home—back to my NOLA. I headed over to the Berry-Picker House before we were to go to the train terminal. I remember feeling like I was in a trance. I took a pencil out of my pocketbook and left a message on the wall of the Berry-Picker House. The same wall that previous berry-pickers had signed over the years while they were staying there during the harvesting seasons. I knew Phillip was gone and would never be able to read my little message, but I left it there all the same. "Phillip, many years ago, I had a son I chose to give up. When I met you, it was somewhat like meeting my own son. Over the years and through our letters you became the son that I never had the pleasure of knowing. I will hold you close to my heart."

In thinking back on the message I left, I realized that I had to get over my self-imposed feelings of not doing enough to find my son so many years ago. I did not choose to give him up! That choice was forced upon me when I was so very young and I just couldn't do anything about it. When you are that young, you just don't know how to deal with the cards you are dealt, but with time, you learn how to play your hand. I was going for a royal flush. I blurted out, "But now I can and now I will find my son!"

When I finished telling Mr. Baynes about the Berry-Picker House Murder and Trial, I breathed a sigh of relief. I was now an open book—my life story would be out there. I didn't cry or get emotional. I felt cleansed and ready to move on—to move forward with my life. In a way, I felt as though Mr. Baynes had become my confessor just as I was to Phillip.

I also told him that I did notice other different messages that had been written on the wall at the Berry-Picker House on my last day there. There was one little message in the right-hand corner down toward the bottom of the wall that read, "Forgive me father for I have sinned." I told him that haunted me and that I would someday have to go back to the farm and find out who may have been the person who wrote it. I never told Mr. Baynes that I had a feeling it was Phillip who wrote that message. I just had it in the back of my mind that I wanted to try and uncover the story that may go with that little message—it was very intriguing to me. I also longed to know more about Phillip and his childhood. From afar, he was a part of my life for so many years. I really started to think more and more about going back to the farm. I felt like I had unfinished business there that needed tending to.

Mr. Baynes insisted on seeing me back home. I did ask him to not put in his notes that I did know about Carmelita's and Phillip's affair as I had never let Anna know that. I didn't want her to be hurt by that information and at this point it didn't really matter. I told him that was just between Phillip and I and that some things need to be taken to the grave. They in fact were and I wanted to keep it that way. He promised me that he wouldn't. I knew at that point that he and I had become friends. I felt as though he had my back and wouldn't do anything to hurt me in any way.

As we parted ways, he was such a gentleman as he asked if he could hold my hand rather than just have a handshake. I was surprised by his request but felt I owed him that.

"Miss Pierre, you truly are the gem of New Orleans and I am honored to have had the privilege of getting to know you and your life story," he said. "I will do you proud with the article I will write about your struggles and your perseverance. You will be an inspiration to so many." He then kissed my hand and said, "I will see you in around a month. I do have one favor to ask of you though." I said, "What is it Mr. Baynes?" He said, "Could you please call me Greg?"

ACQUIESCENCE

Greg was true to his word. It took around a month before he came to me with his draft of his story about me. He entitled it *The Perseverance of Pierre*. He explained to me that there was still the last part of the article that he needed to write before it would be finalized. He told me that there were some things he needed to tell me that would change my life forever. I speculated on certain things he could possibly be eluding to and I did realize that I needed to start to have acquiescence in my life. Acquiesce means to submit or comply silently or without protest or to agree or consent to something. I needed to do just that with many aspects of my life. I needed to let go of so many things that were long lingering in my body and soul. He asked if I could meet him at Jackson Square. I surmised that he had chosen that location as he knew what it meant to me and how it healed and soothed me.

He had a bottle of whiskey and two glasses for us. He poured us both a drink and said, "Miss Pierre, I found out some things that I think are going to upset you, but you need to know them and I am the person who has to tell you." He explained that after our last meeting, he went and did interviews with many people I had talked about during our interviewing process. He was most interested in finding out information about Frankie. I had told him the year that Frankie was killed in the roofing accident and he was able to use that in his investigation. Also, with that information, he was able to go back and find out that Frankie's sister Kim had a box of Frankie's private papers and a few of his pieces of clothing and keepsakes. He asked her if he could look through the box. He knew that Kim and her family could use some extra money so he offered her $100 for the contents of the box. She accepted his offer. In the box there were a few of Frankie's roofing tools, newspaper articles about TCA and a piece of paper that had *Miss Loretta's* written on it attached to a key. Greg said that he did not have the time yet to look into who *Miss Loretta* might have been, but he was still going to investigate that over the next couple of weeks. There was also another document that Greg said he would discuss with me in a few minutes and a copy of a letter to a Father Thomas Mulroney from the Archdiocese of New Orleans. I started to shake a bit when I heard his name like that. Oh, how it stirred up so many memories for me. He went on to tell me that the letter was to formalize that Father Mulroney was being reassigned from New Orleans back to Ireland. It also went on to thank Timothy Anderson and his very generous donation of paying for Father Mulroney's transportation back to Ireland and a small amount of money to help with the expenses for his father's care. Greg went on to speculate that he believed TCA is the one who wanted Father Mulroney out of my life. Greg said that he believed that Father Mulroney would not have left New Orleans or me, if it had not been for TCA's involvement. He just thought that Father Mulroney had no other choice.

Greg said, "I hope this information can offer you some in peace in knowing that Father Tommy may have truly loved you." I let this information sink in for a few minutes. I then said out loud, "I have to let this go and try to not think of what might have been. Things happen for a reason. But Greg, it does my heart good to know that his departure was all orchestrated by others and not because he wanted to leave. I have to believe that he did love me and this information you have given me truly hurts my heart but at the same time will hopefully help to heal this still open wound."

I remembered thinking that I would accept this silently without protest as it would be the only thing I could do to continue on with my life. Greg said that he was pleased with how well I was handling this but that I needed to prepare myself for what he was going to tell me next. One of the other documents he found in Frankie's box was a bank card for Damas DuMonde and a birth certificate of a person named John DuMonde. Greg said that this birth certificate was something that would change my life. He was able to find out that the John DuMonde on the birth certificate was my son. He explained to me that he didn't know why Frankie never shared this information with me. He could only speculate that he was going to tell me, but that he had the accident right around the same time and was never able to get this information to me. With everything he learned about Frankie, he said he just would never believe that he would withhold this information from me. He may have been waiting for the right time to tell me or he may have not actually been able to find out exactly who John DuMonde was or where he was before he died. Greg said he believes that Frankie and Damas DuMonde's paths crossed. He didn't say it out loud, but I could tell by the look on his face that he was thinking the same thing I was, that Frankie was in the brothel the night that Damas was killed. That would explain how Frankie was able to come into possession of the birth certificate of John Du-Monde and Damas' bank card. He may have taken it from Damas that fateful night. There is no way this could ever be proven, but Greg said it seemed the most plausible answer. At this point that didn't matter. The thing that did matter was that because Frankie somehow came into contact with Damas, he was able to get these two documents. If he hadn't, Greg never would have found the documents in Frankie's box of personal effects.

"Oh my God, Greg! What are you saying?" My heart was pounding and I was shaking my head back and forth trying to understand what exactly he was saying. Greg went on to explain he did some digging and found out that the person who the birth certificate belonged to would be around 49 years old. He discovered that Damas had actually had my child, his child, looked after by his placage wife. The boy was never actually put up for adoption. In some circles, placage was a recognized extralegal system in French and Spanish slave colonies by which ethnic European men entered into the equivalent of a common-law marriage with non-Europeans of African and mixed-race descents. Even though it was not legally binding at the time of their arrangement, he did provide the woman, whose name was Jennifer Lacoste, with financial support and a home.   Apparently, Damas would come back to New Orleans often. It was during those times that he was frequenting the houses of ill repute. There is no way to know if Jennifer Lacoste even actually knew exactly who Damas Dumonde was, or if she knew he had a plantation back in Mississippi and the extent of his wealth. It seems he did still stay in a placage relationship with her for quite a few years. However, when Damas was killed in the accident at the brothel and his money was no longer coming her way, she did not want to take care of Damas' child any longer. He was just another mouth to feed. She had enough humanity to still keep a roof over his head and see to his basic needs, but he was not loved. The boy was left on his own most of the time—he was discarded. Greg said that there did seem to be some source of financial support coming into her home from somewhere because she never worked and was able to stay in the same house that she shared with "D". He was able to find out about Jennifer's finances by going to the bank that was listed on "D's" bank card. He offered the Bank Manager $100 to look into the bank account of Mr. Damas DuMonde. There were regular withdrawals from his account to Jennifer Lacoste right up until the time of his death. He found out that Jennifer passed away around twenty years ago so he was not able to actually talk to her. Greg reached for my hand and said, "Miss Pierre, I know where your son is. He is alive and he is well."

I couldn't believe what he was telling me. After all of these years of heartache and pain, I may actually have a chance of seeing my son? I said, "Greg my mind is reeling and I have so many questions for you."

"Miss Pierre, I am going to leave you alone for a few minutes so you can let all of this news sink in," Greg said. "I will be back shortly."

At first, I didn't want him to go, but I realized he was right. This was my time to prepare myself to move forward, but I had to first forgive so many people for the unfairness I felt that they bestowed upon me. So many thoughts were running wild in my mind. I got up from the bench and I did the same pivotal exercise that I did when I first arrived in New Orleans. My life played out in my mind as I circled around seven times. This time when I opened my eyes, I was facing toward Greg who was walking up to me with Johnny from the band. I thought how odd that was that he just ran into him and that he was at Jackson Square at the same time we were. As they approached me, I saw that Johnny was crying and he was carrying a bouquet of pink roses. I was so confused. I thought my God what has happened? I said to Johnny, "Are all our band members okay? Oh no, has something happened to Tee or Maria? Johnny didn't respond. When Greg and Johnny were finally standing within my arm's reach, Greg simply said, "Miss Pierre, I want you to meet your son."

I stood there staring at Johnny and didn't understand what Greg had just said. Before I could ask him, he said, "Miss Pierre, I pondered the best way to tell you that the Johnny you have known since he was a young man, who has grown into the fine man that he is, is indeed your son. I would never have put you in this situation if I were not absolutely sure. I would never play with your heart and emotions like that."

I just looked at Johnny. "Do you believe this to be true?"

"I do and I could think of no other greater gift that I could be given than to learn that you are my mother," Johnny said. "I believe Greg as he told me the entire background of how he found out that I belong to you."

Johnny then handed me the roses that he told me had hand picked from gardens around the city on his way over to meet me. It was such an exhilarating feeling yet awkward at the same time. I actually got dizzy and said I had to sit down. Johnny led me back to the bench. He sat on one side and Greg sat on the other side. We all just sat there looking straight ahead. Greg stayed only long enough to make sure I was okay. He said that he had to be going as Johnny and I had much talking to do and that it should be done in private without him there. He said, "You and Johnny need to heal each other." He told me he would get in contact with me in a week. He had much work to do to get the introductory article to press. He asked me to please read over his draft of the *The Perseverance of Pierre* and to get back to him in a week if possible. He said if there were any things I didn't like, they could be changed or deleted before it went to press. He asked me if he could include in the article that my search for my son had come full circle? If so, it would take him a week to write the ending for the article—now that it could be written.

I replied, "Of course, there is nothing else that could make my life story more complete than that and it is because of you Greg that I have been given this gift. Words cannot express my gratitude for all you have done for me. Please know that I will never forget this."

I explained to him that I did want to discuss all of this at a later time in greater detail but for now, I only wanted to think of getting to know my son. I couldn't believe I was actually talking about spending time with my son! I never thought those words would ever hold true or belong to me. Greg politely took my hand in his and then embraced me. He then discreetly walked away from us. I always imagined that if I ever did find my son, that I would want to hug and hold him so tightly and never let him go. But the feeling I had sitting next to him on the bench was more a feeling of awe. How was it that I was so blessed to have created such a beautiful, talented man? We sat there in silence for a few minutes, both just taking in the closeness of our hearts being so near to each other. I was surprised that I didn't start crying when Greg first said he was my son. But now sitting here with him, I was afraid to look at him as that might wake me from my dream, if this indeed was a dream. When I found the courage to turn to face him, I simply said, "my boy." The natural embrace just happened and the tears just started to flow. Tears of total joy and contentment. I was simply sitting next to my son on a bench in Jackson Square. There was no place in heaven or on earth I would rather have been. God had heard all my prayers and all my prayers had been answered. I had everything I could ever want. I spent the next couple of days talking with Johnny when we could find the free time. We were both so hungry for each other's company and to be near to each other. There were so many questions I had for him about his life growing up since I then knew the circumstances of his childhood. I hoped there would be many conversations between the two of us over time. But right then, I didn't want to overwhelm him. I just wanted us to be in our moment. Our long, awaited moment.

News spread quickly through the Quarter that Johnny was my son. So many people came to me with heartfelt goodwill wishes, especially the CC's. They were always there for me. It was the most wonderful time of my life, but I still had feelings of discontent. I took a piece of paper and decided to make a list of all of the positive and negative things in my life. I started on the left side with all of the positives. Johnny was at the top. Right under him I put down Tee and my granddaughter Maria. Johnny and Tee had a daughter they named Maria. I thought it was so amazing how it turned out that she and I shared the same first name!   They brought precious Maria into the world and into my heart.   Next, I put down that I was still in relatively good health and that my voice was still strong. I continued on and put down *Lace Around the Moon* and how the song was more successful than I ever dreamed. I had received another royalty check that month from the sales of my song. My last positive was that I was blessed to have the friends I had in my life. My friends truly were the guiding and nurturing force behind my many successes.

On the right side of my piece of paper I put down the things that I needed to acquiesce to, the things that were negative in my life that I needed to let go of. Those included Sister Veronica never letting me know that my son was not given up for adoption, but that he was here in New Orleans the entire time and had been living with Jennifer Lacoste and "D" for all of those years many years ago.   Over the past couple of days, I spent a lot of time pondering why she never told me. I believe in my heart that she originally agreed to letting my son be with "D's" placage wife because he must have made it financially beneficial for the Ursuline Convent.   She never would have done it for her own gain. I had heard many years ago through Miss Margaret that the convent was financially struggling back when I was sent there. There just wasn't enough money to take care of all the young women who came there for the reasons I did and the others who came there because they were just cast aside and had nowhere else to go. I also think that she had deliberations of taking his "hush money". I speculated "D" gave it to her for my care while I was there. When I originally was sent to the Ursuline Convent, Sister Veronica had no idea who my child's father was. However, when she learned about my ravaging, she then knew exactly who the father of my child was. I think she came to think of herself as Robin Hood—someone who took from the rich to give to the poor. I think she worked it out in her mind that by her offering me a way out of the abuses of "D", she absolved herself of some of the guilt she felt for taking his tainted money.

The next item on the right side of my list was that I had to get over why Frankie never told me any of the information he had about Father Tommy or about Johnny. In retrospect, I think that Frankie may have been jealous of Father Tommy as he knew of our connection and he may have feared there was a possibility that Father Tommy and I could have developed a serious relationship. That made me think that perhaps Frankie had hoped for the same thing with me. I also had to remember that Frankie worked for TCA and it was TCA who actually had Father Tommy sent back to Ireland. Perhaps they both were in love with me in their own way? As for Frankie, I chose to believe that he was going to tell me about Johnny, but as

Greg had said, he might have died right around the time he found out and just never had the opportunity to tell me. Or perhaps, he didn't have it all figured out by the time he passed.

The last negative thing in my life that I had to let go of was the ravaging of "D". I found it interesting how I thought to myself that if they never happened, I wouldn't have all the wonderful things I had in my life, all the things on the left side of my paper. I thought that just like the beautiful roses Johnny had brought to me on several occasions and the grapes that are harvested each year back at the farm, that perhaps we all have to be cut back or pruned to make it possible for the beautiful flowers to continue to bloom and the grapes to continue to grow year after year. It is a process of renewal. The things that happened to me had to happen in order for me to flourish and grow. I crossed that item off of the list. Things happen for a reason... if you believe. My list was now finalized and I said to myself, "Unfrozen."

I took my piece of paper with me to Jackson Square. I carefully perforated the paper, gently folded up the left side and put it into my brassiere for safekeeping. I then took the right side and carefully ripped it into tiny little pieces. So tiny that you could hardly even recognize that it was even paper. When I had the sheet of paper emulsified, I put it into a little pile. I scooped up the tiny pieces in my hand and walked back to the same place where I started off many years ago. This time instead of spinning around with my eyes closed and wondering where I would wind up facing – what direction my life would take, I stood staunchly steadfast and raised my hand holding the little pieces and threw them into the air. I watched them as they delicately scattered into the wind as I said, "I have let go, I am in total control of my life and I accept all of these things with acquiescence."

With all of that behind me, it was now time to start to make plans to go back to Naples. I needed to smell the grapes again and I needed to reconnect with Anna. Anna had become family to me in the time I got to know her when I was there for Phillip's trail. I wanted Anna to meet my newly found family. I wanted Johnny, Tee and Maria to experience the most wonderful place in the world to me, next to New Orleans. Since I had the financial stability to make this all happen, I would approach my family with this invitation. Since it was the fall, the Lagniappe Orchestra could take a break for the week so that Johnny could be free to accept my proposal. I would also take care of the lost wages the other band members would have as a result of my selfish indulgence of wanting my people with me for a week of heart, body and soul healing.

With my newly found unwavering attitude, there was one other thing I needed to do to totally let go of my past and move forward with my new hopes and dreams for the future. I also needed to do it before going back to Naples. I wanted to move onto the next chapter of my life by closing all of the open doors. I needed to go and pay my respects to TCA. But before I could do that, I needed to speak to Flordie. I hadn't seen her in a very long time. I didn't think much about us not running into each other or why she never tried to contact me after I went to her house that day when her husband said she had gone to see her sister. But then I started to think that perhaps there was a reason she kept her distance. I wasn't going to let this go by. There were still so many of those unanswered questions I had since the time Chester came to speak to me about TCA. I resolutely went to her house and asked her if she would be willing to go with me to his crypt. I thought she would be surprised by my request, but she just looked me straight in my eyes and said, "Pierre I knew this day would be coming, I just didn't know when." I asked her what she meant by that, but said she would explain it all to me at the cemetery.

When we arrived there, we went into the little office building and sure enough, Richard the Groundskeeper was there. He looked so genuinely pleased to see me. "Miss Pierre, it is wonderful to see you again and Miss Flordie, it is always a pleasure," he said. "What can I do for you ladies?" I explained to him that we wanted to go and pay our last respects to TCA at his gravesite. Richard said, "I would be honored if you would allow me to walk you ladies over there." I told him I would really appreciate that as I wasn't quite sure exactly where it was. However, Flordie said, "That won't be necessary Richard, I will take us over there."

I thought it was a bit odd that Flordie knew exactly where the crypt was and that Richard knew her by name. Flordie led the way over to TCA's crypt. We did not speak a word to each other.

I ran my hand over his name etched in the stone and softly sang some of *Lace Around the Moon* for him one last time. I had a wave of peace overcome me and I kissed his name and said a prayer for his soul. Flordie was seated on the little bench that was still there. She asked me to please come over and sit by her.

She just stared straight ahead as she said, "There are some things you need to know. The most importantly being that I was TCA's silent mistress for many years."

I let what she just said register and I was surprised when I blurted out, "Flordie, I am again floored by you. I never once suspected you and TCA had a relationship. But now I am starting to think of little things that maybe now make more sense to me."

I couldn't believe what I was hearing, but I still had to push forward to find out more. I said, "When you put on the Irish wake for Frankie, I thought that TCA assumed you did it for me. But now, I have to ask you, did you do that for him? I know it really doesn't matter, but I want to know."

Flordie dropped her head and she seemed like she was gathering strength before she could respond to me or perhaps she was just weighing her words. She replied, "I did it for both of you. I knew how much Frankie meant to both of you and I couldn't think of a better way to show you both how much you meant to me. It was my gift to both of you—TCA thinking it was for him, and you thinking I did it for you. It is such a strange thing to love two people so much. I loved him desperately, and I love you effortlessly. You have such generosity and an open heart. I was spellbound by you. You say that I floored you on many occasions. You need to know that you did the same to me. I am somewhat of a selfish woman, but you are not. Pierre, didn't you ever wonder why I just showed up at your door step one day and invited myself and the four YP's into your life? It wasn't by chance. It was an orchestrated arrangement. He orchestrated it. I always assumed that he thought there could be a chance that Chester, Faith, Johnny and Tee may have all been his children. He wanted them to all have a positive influence in their lives and he knew that you would be that to them. We know what the man was involved in. He had an insatiable appetite for women and especially women from whom he reaped financial rewards. Many women with whom he had a sexual relationship over the years would come to him and say that they were pregnant with his child. There was no way to prove it, but he did tell me that he always provided financial assistance to the women of these children. That only reinforced my belief that he must have thought they were his offspring, or why would he have done that? He wasn't a monster Pierre. He was just a very self-absorbed, powerful man, but with a heart. He was a man of mystery to me. But when he spoke to me, held me, loved me, there was nowhere else on earth I wanted to be. As you know Pierre, I am a married woman with children of my own. My husband is a good man and I could never do anything to ruin our marriage or his good name. He did nothing wrong. His only fault in my eyes was that he wasn't TCA. There was no way I could ever leave my husband and quite honestly, TCA never even offered me a place at his side if I were to have left my husband. Unfortunately for me, the only person who truly ever could consume his heart was you. I knew that all these years, Pierre. I had to live my life knowing that every day. I held a place in his bed for many years, but I could never gain entrance into the one place I really wanted to be—in his heart. But I never resented you for that. I knew that you were not with him in that way. He once told me that to really love someone is not to set them free, but to never make them your own. I knew he was talking about you, but I never dared say that to him as I didn't want to ruin the one sided love affair we had. I was consumed with him and he was good to me in his own way. Just not the way I craved."

I just sat there for a few moments while I gathered my thoughts. I wasn't mad at her. I was just confused. I realized she never had to tell me any of this, but I think she wanted to make peace with herself. Neither one of us said anything for a few minutes. That gave me the time I needed to formulate the nagging question that was in the back of my mind and now on my tongue.

"Flordie, did TCA know that Johnny was my child all that time? Is that why he had you include him in with the other children when you first came to meet me?

Flordie didn't weigh her words this time when she replied, "I was just as surprised as everyone was when we all found out that Johnny was your son. So, obviously Johnny wasn't his son. Knowing all of this now, it doesn't make sense why he provided financial assistance to Johnny's mother. I thought he did that to the mothers of the YP's because he thought that they could be his children. I can now only speculate that he might have known Johnny was yours and by his looking out for him by giving his mother financial assistance, he may have thought he was doing it for you in some strange, convoluted way. Pierre, I will be honest and say, I just don't know. And unfortunately, you and I will never know the answer to that question."

I told Flordie that this was all too much to comprehend and that I needed some space. I asked her to please leave and ask Richard to come back for me in thirty minutes. Flordie started to cry and said, "Please Pierre, don't be mad at me. I couldn't bear it if our friendship would end because you now know all of this information. I never betrayed you in any way. I just never told you the things I knew or speculated to know."

I thought about it for a minute and said to her, "Flordie, I am hurt and confused. I can't help but feel that I was played by both you and TCA. But I realize it wasn't done for any malicious reasons. I will just need some time to take this all in and make some sense out of it, but I promise, our friendship is still intact. You have done so many wonderful things for me over the many years we have known each other. I thought that a few days ago I let go of all of the things I needed to acquiesce to in my life – the things I needed to get over. I will just have to let go of this as well. But I hope there are not any more of these upsets in my life. I think I have had more than my fair share."

I sat there for a few minutes by myself. I couldn't even think any more. My mind was spent. I composed myself and was drawn over to the next crypt—my crypt. I hadn't allowed myself to think about the fact that it may be mine as I thought it was all rather morbid to be thinking about my death. However, I also needed to find out if it really was mine and what I would need to do to get the paperwork showing my ownership of it. I was very surprised when I looked at the front of the crypt, it had a word added in between "My" and "Angel". The word was "Beloved." When I went back into the office building, Richard handed me an envelope with my name typed on it. He said, "Miss Pierre, I had hoped you would come back one day for this." I asked him if he minded if I sat down at the desk to read whatever was in the envelope? He pulled out a chair for me and I opened up the envelope. Inside was a legal document showing ownership of the plot and crypt with the number assigned to it. The documents looked official and stated that "Maria Pierre Quinones is the owner of such plot and crypt."

There it was, the proof that I needed to confirm my suspicions that TCA knew exactly who I was all this time. I never told a living soul my real surname. I didn't think that even sister Veronica knew it was Quinones. I then believed that TCA knew that Johnny was my son. I caught myself from pondering this even further. None of this made any difference now. There was a cover sheet that further identified the lawyer's office I would need to go to if and when I would take ownership of the crypt, but that was all that was in the envelope. I was hoping there would be a note or something personal from TCA explaining things to me, but there wasn't. I just sat there speechless and couldn't even say anything more to Richard. He made it easier for me when he said, "Miss Pierre you hopefully will have quite some time before you need to finalize any of these documents. Just take the envelope with you and think things through. It is not any of my business, but I believe *someone* really loved you."

I remember thinking that those words on my crypt were the words TCA could never say to me during his lifetime, he could only say them to me in his death.

When I finally arrived back home at my cottage, I just sat at my kitchen table. I couldn't even fathom having a whiskey. I just sat there thinking for a long while. If it were true that TCA was the father to Chester, Faith and Tee, that would be something I would never tell Tee. It would make no difference in her life at this point. It just didn't matter. She had a wonderful husband and a beautiful daughter. Why subject her to these rumors. But I remember thinking that there were so many secrets, so many lies and all just to disguise the truths he tried to hide. I thought to myself what a complicated, convoluted man he was. I did love him and I did loathe him. He was gone and all his secrets died with him. Just as he was in his final resting place, I too needed to put all of this to rest.

THE MIRROR

As Greg had requested, I finally made the time to read *The Perseverance of Pierre*. I had to digest it all in private. It was quite odd to see my life story on the paper typed on a typewriter. It was an incredulous feeling. I have to admit I felt pride when I finally finished reading his article. I tried to step back and read it without bias, but I realized that would not be possible. So, I read through it again and read it with an open heart—my open heart. I only made a few minor changes to Greg's draft. After they were done, I went to bring them to him at the *New Orleans Observer* where he was working. When I arrived there, I was taken aback by the outpouring of admiration and respect I was treated with by his colleagues. They all wanted to meet me and shake my hand. Greg asked me to please have a seat at his desk. His desk was piled high with papers. It was chaotic organization. I could see his typewriter off to the side. I thought how incredible it was that he was able to take the words I had spoken to him over our several meetings and with his fingers, ink and his creativity with words, he put my story to paper. He had become the epitome of a professional newspaper reporter. However, he took me by surprise when he went into his desk drawer and pulled out a bottle of whiskey and two glasses! I couldn't believe that we were there on his turf and that he had started to keep whiskey, my signature drink in his desk drawer. We had become more than friends—we had bonded. Greg thanked me for my edits and he was very anxious to share some information that he had just learned with me. He told me that he was able to find out some information regarding the key and the piece of paper he found in Frankie's box of personal effects with the name of *Miss Loretta* on it. He looked back into public records and found there was a bawdy house called *Miss Loretta's*, around the early 1900's in Black Storyville. Black Storyville was at the back of Storyville and was the only place where black men could go to for "pleasure." Since Storyville had been closed down for almost 20 years, it took him some digging to find out exactly who Miss Loretta was. It turns out she was a petite, red headed woman, who was previously a "comfort woman" before becoming the saloon owner of her namesake. People who misjudged her small stature and tried to cause chaos in her establishment, were quickly met by a switchblade knife she would keep in her ample bosom. Patrons quickly learned not to mess with Miss Loretta, if they wanted to keep their parts intact. She had a reputation as a savvy business owner. She was willing to open up shop in an area that did not have the opulence of most of the houses in Storyville. She catered to the cast-off clientele and became known as *Loving Loretta*, but they nicknamed her *Double L*. She accepted those who were not able to walk through the white area of Storyville into her saloon and treated everyone who came to her bar wood with the respect and dignity they were not granted streets up. She saw the color of money and not the color of skin. Greg was also able to find out that when Storyville ended, Miss Loretta moved to Algiers on the West Bank of the Mississippi. That is where he found her. She was running a very upscale supper club called, *Jewels*. He went there and was able to meet her. He said she was at first a bit resistant to speak to him. He explained to her that he found her name on a piece of paper with a key attached to it that was in Frankie Quigley's box of personal effects and he wanted to know if she could shed any light on why her name and this key would have been there? I told her that I was a friend of yours and was only trying to obtain this information for you. When she heard that I was there on your behalf, she eventually warmed up to me and offered me a drink. She also poured herself one and came from behind the bar and sat down next to me. She actually breathed a sigh, looked me in the eyes and said, "I have not heard Frankie's name brought up in quite some time. Some things you just try to keep out of your mind and heart. I mean you no offense as you seem like a nice young man, but this is none of your business. I will never speak a word to you about anything pertaining to Frankie or that key. But you can pass along to your friend, Miss Pierre that if she wants to know things, she will have to come and speak to me herself. Let's just say, I would be willing to unlock the truth to her and only her."

Greg said "So there you have it. I won't be able to assist you any further with finding out what information Miss Loretta may have as she will only speak to you. You will need to go and see her yourself if you feel you need to know what the key is for and what her association with Frankie was all about."

We went over the draft and I pointed out the changes to Greg. When we were done, he poured us each a drink. We both just sat there for a few moments in silence looking at each other and sharing a drink. I finally broke the silence and said, "You have done me proud. Thank you!" I left shortly after that as I had another stop I had to make. I did think that after I returned from my trip to Naples, I would get in touch with Miss Loretta. Since she seemed to know who I was, perhaps she would have some information that could be pertinent to me. I was intrigued by the key that was in Frankie's box of keepsakes and wanted to know exactly what she meant when she told Greg that she would unlock the truth to me. But for now, I had other places I needed to be.

I went back to Jackson Square before leaving on my trip, the place my story actually started at. I thought back to that pivotal night when I was in Jackson Square asking God to set my direction, my destiny. Here it was nearly 50 years later. How things had changed and time had passed, not in a blink of an eye, but rather in a slow batting of an eye. I reflected on my life that had passed behind me. I realized how fortunate I was to still be alive. I had lived a hard, purposeful life. I had helped others because I was so appreciative to those who helped me along my path. I got up from the park bench and walked along the side of Jackson Square over to St. Louis Cathedral. I knew it would be a few weeks before I would be back there, but I was looking forward to my new ventures. I stopped in and lit a candle and said a prayer—a prayer of thanks.

In less than a year of my leaving Naples, I was headed back there. The circumstances of my return visit were ones I never had thought would happen, not even in my wildest of dreams. Johnny, Tee, Maria, Greg Baynes and myself were sitting in a private section of the train. Maria was sitting right beside me. I just never wanted her to be out of my sight, out of my arm's reach. How blessed I was to not only have found my son, but to have also learned that I had a granddaughter! I turned my face to look out the window as the train moved along its tracks. I was so surprised to see the person looking back in the glass pane was beaming. I was no longer gaunt and haggard looking as I was when I first returned from Naples. I had blossomed and looked healthy, happy and content. I closed my eyes for a bit and tried to relax. I was very excited about seeing Anna and just being back at the farm. I was also excited about how Johnny, Tee and I were moving forward so quickly with the music for *Christmas Dishes*. I always knew I would turn my poem into a song and I couldn't believe how Johnny and Tee embraced working on the song with me. They wanted to be involved in every aspect of it. We originally started out with me singing the song. However, I started thinking more and more of asking Tee to do a duet of the song with me. I hadn't told her that yet as we were still trying to write the music and have the words fit in. There would be time for all of this when we were in Naples for the week. I had a feeling that would be where many things would come together for me in this new phase of my life. I was able to doze off for a bit and for the first time in a long time, I didn't dream. I simply had peace.

The articles that ran in the *New Orleans Observer* that Greg had done on my life story were very well received. It made Greg really stand out amongst his peers in the newspaper industry. He was able to convince the editor of the paper that there was more to my story, but he would need to go back to Naples to be able to look into all the unanswered questions about Phillip and the Berry-Picker Murder Trial. The people in New Orleans became captivated with the trial and wrote letters to Greg and the *Observer* asking for more articles on the subject and on me. Greg would be doing several articles while he was with me in Naples. It was like a cross-country connection between the two cities. Naples, New York, and New Orleans, Louisiana, were becoming sister cities!

Anna had offered for us all to stay in the big house at the farm for the duration of our visit. She explained there was a new farm manager named Gene, who was staying in one of the rooms, but that there was plenty of room in the house for all of us. I explained to her through letter writing that I appreciated the offer, but with the large brood of my people, I thought it would be best for us to stay at the Naples Hotel. Anna had written back that she made reservations for a week for all of us at the Naples Hotel. However, she said that if we decided to stay on longer, she would have to insist that we stay at the big house at the farm. She explained in her letter writing that although she still owned the farm, she turned over all aspects of the farm management to the new farm manager. People in Naples still had feelings of animosity toward Anna over the entire situation of Phillip killing Carmelita. She said things were improving with time but she still kept herself a bit off in the distance. She understood why people felt the way they did. After all, she was Phillip's twin and this entire ordeal changed the little town of Naples in many ways. She just said that she needed to go on. What else could she do?

Anna and Peter, Anna's husband, both had an automobile at the train station to pick us up and take us to the Naples Hotel. Anna and I embraced and held on to each other for dear life. We both were crying and relished in this moment of reconnection. Greg and myself went with Anna. Johnny, Tee and Maria went with Peter. I was so happy to see that on the way to the Naples Hotel, both automobiles pulled into the farm. We all got out and stretched our legs. It was again harvesting season and I was transcended into another time when I first took in the aromatic smell of the grapes. A tear spilled down my cheek. It was a tear for Phillip and for all things that might have been. We only stayed there for a few minutes overlooking the beautiful little vineyard. It was very odd to me that I had the feeling that I was home. I thought to myself, how could that be when New Orleans had become my home. But I just couldn't dismiss this feeling. Anna said we needed to be heading over to the hotel. She just wanted us to see it for a minute so that Greg, Johnny, Tee and Maria could have a first-time experience of what the farm was all about. She assured all of us that we would be spending as much time there as our schedule would allow. I didn't say anything to anyone on our ride to the hotel. But I started to think more and more that perhaps I would be staying on here for a bit longer than the week I had planned on. We all had return train tickets for a week later. However, I didn't have any commitments that I couldn't cancel or postpone for the next few weeks. Maybe I would take Anna up on her invitation and stay on longer. That would definitely give me more time to look into the little message that was written on the wall of the Berry-Picker House and to just spend time with Anna learning all about her and Phillip's upbringing with their family.

We all continued on our way and we were all dropped off in front of the hotel. Anna said that she had a room for us in the back so that we could all have a meal together. Peter took care of having all of our luggage placed in our rooms. We had a total of three rooms. One for myself, one for Greg and one for Johnny, Tee and Maria. When we all walked into the back room, I couldn't believe how beautifully it was decorated with several different colored roses! I didn't recall ever telling Anna how much I loved roses, so I speculated that Johnny and Greg must have told her. I was so touched by the gesture of all of these beautiful roses in different vases. Their scent was intoxicating and to me, the roses never smelled as sweet as they did then. As we were eating our wonderful dinner, I heard *Lace Around the Moon* playing in the background. It was so natural how all of my people in the room started to sing along. I also joined in. I was taken aback when I heard one of the voices rising above all of the others. It was Maria's! Her voice was so rich and deep yet had an innocence to it all at the same time. I immediately thought that my song *Christmas Dishes* could be sung by myself, Tee and Maria—it could be a trio. My life had come full circle in so many ways. Everything that I had always wanted for myself had actually happened. I didn't think there could be anything more wonderful that could happen in my life.

Right while dessert was being served, a woman walked into the room and walked over to Anna and Peter. She was carrying two very young babies, one in each arm. Anna came over to my seat carrying the little one in pink. She took me by the hand and asked me to stand up as she put the child in my arms. Peter came over with the little one in blue. She said "Pierre, there are some people we want to introduce you to. I would like you to meet little Phillip and little Pierre."

ABOUT THE AUTHOR

Mary Pierre Quinn-Stanbro is from Buffalo, NY and currently resides there. She is married to Gene Stanbro and plans to move to the Gene-Pierre Vineyard in Naples, NY when she retires in 2019 from her Federal Government career where she has pro-vided thirty-four years of public service. Mary Pierre is writing her Sequel to "Lace Around the Moon" and "The Berry-Picker House." It is called "The Grape Farm." After that, she will be writing her next Novella called "The Band of Blue." It is about a fictional murder which takes place in Buffalo back in the late 1950's. It is a dedication to the Buffalo Police Department and her father and grandfather who were both Buffalo Police Officers. Mary Pierre has an Associate's Degree from Trocaire College and a Bachelor's Degree from Buffalo State College. She has always wanted to share her writings with others and is blessed to be doing so.

73483752R00105

Made in the USA
Columbia, SC
11 September 2019